"YOU CHEATED ME!"

"Son, you'd best be careful how you use words like that. Say them to the wrong fellow and they can wind up caught in your throat, y' know?"

"I say you cheated, damn you," Ben cried loudly. He sprang to his feet angrily. Behind him, the room full of tipplers and friendly card players scrambled to get out of the way.

"I don't want t' hurt you, boy. Go home now, and next time don't insist on bein' stupid." Longarm reached out with his left hand, slowly, and picked up an empty shot glass the man to his left had been using. "Here," he said softly. He tossed the glass to the kid. Amber liquor sprayed high into the air. So, maybe the glass hadn't been empty after all.

Ben looked startled and, out of automatic reflex, moved to catch the glass.

When he looked up again he stared all the harder. But this time into the gaping muzzle of Longarm's .45. No one in the place, including Ben, had so much as seen Longarm's hand move.

If he needed an excuse to walk away, he damn sure had one now . . .

TABOR EVANS

**AND THE
GRAND SLAM HEIST**

J

JOVE BOOKS, NEW YORK

LONGARM AND THE GRAND SLAM HEIST

A Jove Book / published by arrangement with
the author

PRINTING HISTORY
Jove edition / May 1996

All rights reserved.
Copyright © 1996 by Jove Publications, Inc.
This book may not be reproduced in whole
or in part, by mimeograph or any other means,
without permission. For information address:
The Berkley Publishing Group, 200 Madison Avenue,
New York, New York 10016.

The Putnam Berkley World Wide Web site address is
http://www.berkley.com

ISBN: 0-515-11861-3

A JOVE BOOK®
Jove Books are published by The Berkley Publishing Group,
200 Madison Avenue, New York, New York 10016.
JOVE and the "J" design are trademarks
belonging to Jove Publications, Inc.

PRINTED IN THE UNITED STATES OF AMERICA

10 9 8 7 6 5 4 3 2 1

AND THE
GRAND SLAM HEIST

Chapter 1

Lordy but this heat was awful, the worst Longarm could remember in . . . hell, it was just plain the worst he could remember. Period.

Looking down Colfax Avenue toward the gold-domed state capitol building he could actually see the shimmering rise of heat off the cobblestones of the paving.

There hadn't been any rain in weeks, maybe months. He supposed there was someone who kept track of such things. The thing he knew for sure on the subject was that it had been a helluva long while.

Still and all, there was relief in sight.

The service of routine subpoenas is something anyone is capable of doing and usually is a chore to be avoided. It is dreary, uneventful, and entirely uninteresting work.

But right now it sounded mighty attractive to United States Deputy Marshal Custis Long.

And just as quick as he got to the office this morning he intended to exercise his privileges as the senior deputy— well, at least the most senior one in town at this particular moment in time—to nab the job of serving papers in the matter of the Department of Justice versus John J. Bidwell.

Not that the case itself was all that interesting. Not hardly.

The *United States v. Bidwell*—according to what little Longarm knew of it—had to do with the alleged infringement of right and title to a mining claim. It was all technical as hell and about as dull as the law was capable of getting.

Which, in fact, was pretty damned dull.

The reason Longarm wanted the assignment had nothing to do with the case itself.

It was the fact that all the witnesses and participants were in Leadville, up near the headwaters of the Arkansas River.

And that meant those folks all lived at something like eleven thousand feet of elevation.

Down here in Denver, at a mere mile above sea level, the heat was unbearable.

But up in the high country they hadn't ever seen a hot summer day. Longarm's own personal experience was that a fella could damn near freeze his nuts off if he forgot his coat on an August evening. He'd seen snow there the last week of July once and knew for a fact that the residents claimed it was impossible to get garden plants to bear because of the cold nights even through the summer months.

The highest temperature he'd heard of in the town was something in the upper 70s, and the high 60s or low 70s were common summer afternoon highs.

Yeah, Leadville sounded like just about the best place he could think of right now.

And if some other deputy thought he was gonna pull that plum out of the pot and claim it for himself, well, Longarm would just jolly well pull rank.

He'd had enough of this heat for one lifetime, thank you.

He reached the front steps of the granite-walled Federal Building and mounted them, grateful for the shade indoors and the resulting impression—not necessarily accurate—of coolness that accompanied the darker surroundings.

He passed a gaggle of twittering schoolgirls in the hallway. And couldn't help but smile—carefully though so they couldn't see—when after he'd passed he overheard one of them make a sound like she was fixing to swoon, that being quickly followed by a bunch of giggling and laughing.

Well, he took it as a compliment anyway and walked just a little taller.

2

Not that he had any interest in a bunch of high school–age children. After all, little fish belong in the pond until they're big enough to eat.

But a fellow couldn't help but be pleased when a total stranger offered a mite of admiration.

Longarm couldn't see the attraction himself. Hell, he was just another male. A little taller than most, perhaps, with broad shoulders and a horseman's narrow-hipped build. He had brown hair, brown eyes, and a large but tidy sweep of dark brown mustache.

He wore a flat-crowned brown Stetson hat, corduroy trousers tucked into black stovepipe cavalry boots, and, despite the weather, a lightweight coat. His customary vest had been discarded, however, until the damned weather broke, which meant he also had to leave behind his usual watch chain . . . the one that had a brass-framed derringer brazed in place where a fob would ordinarily be.

Not that he was weaponless. He carried a double action .45 Colt revolver in a cross-draw rig just to the left of his belt buckle. And a four-shot Sharps Gambler in .32 caliber was in the watch pocket of his britches to make up for the lack of his old reliable derringer.

He himself considered his facial features to be rather ordinary if weathered and wrinkled some. But there were a fair number of ladies who, like those school girls, found him more attractive than the average Joe.

It was not a situation that he complained about overmuch.

The simple truth was that Custis Long was satisfied with his lot in life.

There wasn't a thing he really needed that he didn't have . . . a fair amount that he *wanted* but lacked, perhaps, but nothing that he actually needed . . . and nothing that he really wanted to do that he wasn't able to accomplish.

Including, by damn, getting out of this miserable heat.

The Bidwell subpoenas would see to that.

He entered the office of the United States Marshal, Denver District, Department of Justice, and draped his Stetson over a peg on the coatrack near Marshal William Vail's private office.

"G'mornin', Henry," he said to the mild-looking but, in fact, bulldog-tenacious clerk who sat at a desk near that door, guarding it as effectively as any dragon could ever have managed.

"Good morning, Custis. You can go on in if you please. He said he has something for you today."

Longarm nodded and marched into Billy Vail's office without the formality of knocking.

Yessir, he'd already checked the train schedule and had his bag packed and ready to go. He could be on a westbound up the South Platte valley by eleven fifteen and into the cool high-country air just a little past lunchtime.

Right at that moment Custis Long was about as happy as a pig in the sunshine.

Chapter 2

"You can't *do* this to me," Longarm moaned. "You *know* I been counting on going t' Leadville this week."

"Now how could I have known a thing like that, Custis?" the balding marshal asked in a soft, patient tone.

"You knew," Longarm insisted, noticing after the words were out of his mouth that his own tone of voice sounded more than a mite petulant. Well, dammit, that was just too bad. Billy Vail did so know Longarm was counting on getting into the high country to escape this heat. They'd talked about it just yesterday afternoon, hadn't they? Or was that somebody else Longarm mentioned the fact to? Not that it really mattered. If Billy Vail hadn't known then he should've guessed. The point was that Longarm was *entitled* to the job of serving those papers in and around Leadville.

"I am truly sorry, Custis, but I've already assigned Maeternick to the Leadville job."

Longarm jumped like the boss just stuck him with a pin. Huh. More than a pin it was, actually. Maeternick? Puhleese! "Billy," he protested with another heartfelt—if somewhat theatrical—groan, "doesn't seniority have any effect at all around here? Ain't I got *any* rights over the tenderfeet an' the wet-ears?" That kid Maeternick, for instance, wasn't hardly old enough to shave. Looked like he oughta still be in high school. Wanted the pretty girls to think he was a grown-up. At least that was how Longarm figured the infant's appointment as a deputy. That and the fact that his daddy was a senator from one of those back-

East states that nobody with hair on his ass would ever want to visit. Longarm rolled his eyes and slouched in his chair and otherwise tried to make known some of the things it wouldn't have been polite to say right out loud.

"Of course seniority entitles you to some privilege, Custis. And next time if you'll just let me know in time so that I can do something about it, perhaps things will turn out differently. In the meantime I have another assignment for you. Something suitable to your talents and experience."

"But I wanta go to Leadville, Billy. You know that."

"Oh, I think you'll find this trip even more interesting," the marshal said. "After all, it isn't like you'll be overworked. In fact, you can look at it as a sort of vacation. Why, it will be *fun*. Honestly."

The red-cheeked marshal smiled, his expression a mask of innocence, and spread his palms wide. Nothing up those sleeves, nosirree-bob.

"A vacation, huh. I've had your kind o' vacation before, Billy, an' if it's all the same to you I'd as leave spend a week stoking a furnace in Hell as take another one of what you call a vacation."

"Custis. Really! You hurt my feelings. When was the last time I. . . ."

"That's when it was, all right," Longarm injected. "Last time you put a hurting on me was the last time."

Vail clucked his tongue and shook his head in a display of great sadness. "I am sorry you feel that way, Custis. Honestly I am." He looked so completely innocent . . . hurt . . . feelings wounded. . . .

Longarm looked at his boss. And thought that maybe, just maybe, this time he was misjudging the man. After all, they were friends. Even good friends. And they'd gotten along mighty well, everything considered, for all this time now. So maybe, just maybe. . . . "What is it you're wantin' me t' do, boss?" he asked.

And knew the question was a damnfool mistake even before the last sound of it was outa his mouth.

6

Chapter 3

"Baseball?" Longarm asked with a groan that he didn't bother to muffle.

"That's right. It's a game, Custis. You play it with a ball and a stick that they call a bat and. . . ."

"Dammit, Billy, I know what it is. It's just. . . ."

"Sit back down there and listen for a minute, will you? Just let me explain."

Longarm shook his head. But he also sat down. He reached into his pocket for a cheroot, pulled it out and went through the routine of trimming and lighting without bothering to ask Billy's permission. Without bothering to offer a smoke to the boss, either.

He couldn't help but sniff and grumble a mite. After all, why should the marshal be pestering a grown man with something about a kid's game when there were papers to be served up in cool, quiet Leadville.

It simply was not fair. Not no way at all.

"Are you listening, Custis?"

"I'm listening, Billy." Longarm grunted once more, sort of to ensure that his point came across, and puffed sullenly on his smoke while the marshal spoke.

"I don't suppose you follow the sporting accounts in the *News*," Billy said by way of a preamble.

Longarm said nothing, just continued to imitate a pufferbelly smokestack.

"No, I didn't really expect that you would. Well, I do, Custis. And I've noticed something. Do you remember that post office robbery in Las Vegas, New Mexico, two months ago?''

Longarm took the cheroot out of his mouth and gave the slightly soggy end of it an accusing glare, then stuffed it back into his jaw and grunted. It was an affirmation. Of sorts.

"There was a bank robbery in Springer, New Mexico, two weeks later and a payroll robbery three weeks after that. Do you recall reading anything about those?''

Longarm frowned in thought for a moment, then asked, "Federal payroll?''

"No, neither of those crimes was in our jurisdiction. The postal theft was, of course, but not the other two.''

"So why . . . ?'' Longarm almost forgot that he didn't want to become interested in any of this, dammit. After all, it was so nice and cool and pleasant up in Leadville.

"Because I happened to notice a coincidence involving those crimes, Longarm. Except that I sincerely doubt there is anything remotely coincidental about them.''

In spite of himself, Longarm cleared his throat. And lifted an eyebrow.

"None of the newspapermen who covered the events made any connection, Custis, and the reports were published at different times . . . something to do with real news traveling faster than news about mere entertainments, I suppose . . . but I noted the locations first and checked the dates afterward.''

"Yes?''

"We seem to have a gang of robbers on the loose who are baseball fans,'' Billy said.

"Pardon me?''

"Yes, well, that may not be the full story, of course.'' Billy smiled and steepled his fingers under his chin while he peered closely at the tall deputy who no longer looked quite so sulky. "My point, Longarm, is that those robberies have been committed in the same communities and at approximately the same times as a series of baseball games.''

"Baseball games,'' Longarm repeated.

8

"That is what I said, yes. A team of professional ball players from Austin, Texas, has been making an extended exhibition tour through New Mexico and the panhandle towns. They played in Clayton, New Mexico, two weeks ago and intend, if I understand their schedule correctly, to swing north into Kansas and then come west into Colorado."

"Is this goin' somewhere, boss?"

"Oh, it is indeed, my impatient friend. It is indeed."

"Would you mind . . . ?"

"May I be candid with you, Longarm?"

"Jeez, Billy, I wish you would."

"I have a hunch."

"You?"

"Me," the marshal confirmed. "And, um, did I or did I not recently overhear you tell a young lady that you once were employed as a pitcher for the Chicago White Stockings?"

"Billy, c'mon. You might've heard me say such a thing. In fact I seem t' recall something o' the sort my own self. But, lord Billy, that don't make it true. I mean . . . a man is permitted some small liberties when it comes t' things said in the heat o' battle. Jeez, Billy, the only thing I've ever pitched is woo. I wouldn't know where t' find the handle on a baseball."

"Oh dear," Billy said. He looked disappointed. No, Longarm decided, the boss looked . . . embarrassed. That was it. The man looked positively, absolutely and downright embarrassed about something here.

"Billy?"

"I am afraid," the marshal said, "that I have already promised Douglas a second string pitcher for his team."

"Boss," Longarm said, "I think there is something that I'm missing in this picture."

"Yes," Vail agreed. "I'm afraid we've both made a few errors this time. Uh, no pun intended."

Longarm blinked a curl of pale smoke out of his eyes.

9

Chapter 4

Longarm felt damn near naked as he stepped off the narrow gauge Plains and Pacific coach at Medicine Lodge, Kansas. He wore his usual .45 and carried a derringer in his watch pocket, but for the first time in a considerable while he'd been forced to leave his Winchester and well-worn old McClellan saddle behind.

Baseball players, after all, have scant need of saddles or of rifles.

Dammit, if there was any way Longarm could have gotten Billy to change his mind. . . . But of course there hadn't been. Too late for that, the boss said. All they could do now was for Longarm to meet this Douglas McWhortle fellow as planned and hope for the best.

And so Longarm had taken a Denver and Rio Grande train south, a Kansas and Pacific eastward, and then the chuff-a-clunk little Plains and Pacific coach south again and now here he was.

But he still would rather be in Leadville, not that anyone else seemed to care.

Medicine Lodge—he'd been there a number of times before—was an uncommonly pretty town with an air of permanence if not of plenty. The thing was the stores and the homes here appeared to belong to folks who actually cared about them. This was no boomtown that would flower briefly and then die. A body could tell that just by looking around.

Which Longarm did for a moment to try and get his bearings.

The downtown consisted of a stone courthouse, a fairly imposing bank made of brick and carved stone trim, a collection of stores selling hats and hardware, groceries and leather goods, plows, pumps, whatever.

There were four saloons and three churches in view from where he stood and, beside the courthouse, a tiny stone building scarcely larger than a backyard shitter that had steel barred windows and a sign over the door reading "Jail." It was a good thing jail is a four-letter word. If they'd tried to post a sign saying "Calabozo" they'd have had to add an extension onto the place just to have room enough for the extra letters.

Not that a simple baseball player would have any interest in the local jail or in the town marshal who ran it.

One thing that Longarm did not see was a place called the Bradley Arms.

Which was where he was supposed to meet McWhortle.

Longarm sighed. The quickest way to get this over with, he figured, was to get it started.

He lit a cheroot, took a fresh grip on his carpetbag, and went in search of the Bradley Arms and of a fellow name of McWhortle.

Douglas McWhortle wasn't at home at the Bradley Arms—despite the fancy name it turned out to be no more than a large boardinghouse—so Longarm parked his carpetbag there in the care of the heavily mustached proprietor—a lady named Mrs. Finney—and followed her directions to where she said McWhortle should be busy working.

Longarm wasn't so sure about it being work the man was doing because all he found in the big field behind the Hope Methodist Church was a bunch of grown men playing at games like so many kids. It didn't much look like work

11

to Longarm. But then what the hell did he know about baseball anyway?

"McWhortle?" he asked the oldest looking fellow in the bunch.

"That man there," the oddly dressed gent responded, pointing to a kid who looked like he was still within hollering distance of his teens.

Every one of this crowd of a dozen or so was dressed in flannel. Flannel britches and flannel shirts and ducky little flannel billed caps so dumb looking that Longarm figured they would be a marvel for anyone wanting to get into some recreational bar fights.

The flannel uniforms had thin stripes running vertically through the cloth of some dark maroon shade. It was at least as hot here as back in Denver and the flannel clothing looked about as cool and comfortable to wear in this weather as so many blast furnaces. The ball players acted like they didn't know any better than to wear flannel clothes in summer. And hell, maybe they didn't. Longarm was commencing to suspect, as if he hadn't had the thought twenty times already, that this was not the best assignment Billy Vail ever gave him. Now if he'd just been up in Leadville. . . .

"You're McWhortle?"

"That I am, mister. What can I do for you?"

Longarm glanced around at all the ball players, most of whom had sidled over close to listen in on what the stranger among them had to say. "Could we have a word in private, please?"

McWhortle gave his boys a wink and a grin but nodded to Longarm and motioned him off to the side. "Get on with the fielding practice while I see what this gentleman wants. Ted, you take the bat. Hit some slow grounders for the infield and when you get tired of that pop some high ones for the outfield."

A lanky redhead with freckles and a nose that looked

12

like it got broken on a pretty regular basis picked up a chunk of wood and a bag of baseballs and waved the rest of the bunch out into the grassy field. McWhortle motioned for Longarm to follow and ambled off toward the shade— mighty damned welcome shade so far as Longarm was concerned—of a small oak in the side yard of the church.

"Now what is it I can do for you, Mister . . . ?"

Longarm introduced himself, and McWhortle began to chuckle. "You're Sergeant Vail's friend then?"

"Marshal Vail, not sergeant," Longarm corrected.

"Oh yes, sorry. I, uh," he grinned, "to tell you the truth, deputy, I mistook you for the local briber."

"I beg your pardon?"

"Of course you wouldn't understand what I'm talking about, would you?"

"I reckon I could agree with that, Mr. McWhortle."

"You see, we are a traveling professional club. Good players, really. Not big league–caliber perhaps, but far and away above the level of the local bumpkins we play against. But more often than you might think there is some local bigwig, usually a blowhard but some of them would surprise you, who thinks local honor must be upheld." The young club manager's grin got all the bigger. "These gents think so strongly about this that they come around just regular as clockwork and offer to bribe us to throw the game."

"An' just how is it that you respond to these offers, Mr. McWhortle?"

The fellow laughed. "We take the money, of course. Whatever they offer. After all, we're in this trying to make a living. And then just as naturally we play our usual game. And usually win, of course."

"An' if the fella who paid you the bribe complains?"

"And admit in public that he paid out a bribe? They won't generally do that. Besides, we make it a point to get out of a town just as quick as we can once a game is over. Among other things it cuts down on fights between our boys and the disgruntled locals.'' McWhortle chuckled. ''It's amazing how testy some of them get after we trounce them on the field. They seem to think a show of manhood is in order. So we've learned to schedule our games so a coach or a train is pulling out within half an hour or so of our game being ended.''

''An' you thought I was one o' these. . . .''

''No offense intended, I assure you. I just didn't expect . . . I mean, I was expecting a ball player, you know. And forgive me if I say this, deputy, but you don't have the look. You aren't—how can I put this?—loose enough. I mean, you look like you might actually take an interest in things other than whiskey and women and baseball.''

It was Longarm's turn to grin. ''I can hold my own with a clear majority o' those things, Mr. McWhortle. If that makes you feel any better. But as for me bein' a ball player, well, there's been a little misunderstanding about that.''

''Hold on a minute, deputy. I have to go chew Caleb's ass off. You can tell me what's going on, and what all you need, soon as I get back.''

Longarm nodded and the youngster—he still looked awfully short in the years department but acted like he was damn sure in charge in spite of that—trotted off to first growl at one of his players and then, much more calmly, teach the man just exactly how McWhortle wanted some small point of play handled.

Longarm stood in the entirely welcome protection of the shade and enjoyed a cheroot while he waited for McWhortle to return.

Chapter 5

"All I really know is that my father-in-law asked me to cooperate with Sergeant Vail. Excuse me, I believe you said that should be Marshal Vail now."

"That's right. But who's your father-in-law?"

"His name is Ed Barnes. My wife is his second daughter Leonore. Mr. Barnes's older brother Maynard used to be in the same Ranger company as the ser—as your marshal."

"An' he asked your daddy-in-law t' ask you t' go along with whatever Billy wanted," Longarm said.

"Something like that, yes. Which I was perfectly happy to do when I was informed that the marshal would supply me with an accomplished pitcher to join the team."

"Yeah, well, I think I explained that," Longarm said sheepishly.

McWhortle laughed. "So you did, deputy. So you did."

"Look, d'you know anything at all about the robberies that've been following along with your team?"

"To tell you the truth, I didn't even know they were happening. As I explained to you before, it's our habit to take our share of the gate and be on the first transportation out of town, preferably as soon as the game ends and certainly before the sun goes down. I had no idea any such robberies took place, although I looked up some old newspapers once I was told about the crimes. Your marshal is absolutely right. There have been at least four such thefts and possibly more. All of them taking place while our games were in progress. Which makes very good sense when you think about it. Our tour is taking us to communities that lack the entertainments available in major cities. People from miles around come to watch us play. Frankly, we count on that. We make our money by taking sixty percent of the gate receipts. The home team pays expenses, if any, and keeps whatever is left. We've found our games so popular in these small towns that virtually everyone who can come does. Stores and businesses close down and usually one or more churches set up food stalls to sell sandwiches and candy and lemonade and the like. We don't ask for any percentage of the charity take, of course.'' McWhortle sighed. ''I hate to think we are being used to the detriment of others.''

''Any ideas on who could be doin' this? Or why?''

'' 'Why' seems easy enough. For the money, of course.''

''I meant, why you an' your boys in particular,'' Longarm said.

''I'm afraid I have no opinion about that.''

''Was the tour laid out beforehand?''

''Oh my yes. We had to plan everything ahead of time so we could make arrangements for the transportation, rooms, meals. We even had to plan our laundry layovers and like that.''

''An' was all this announced? To the public, I mean?''

McWhortle frowned in thought for a moment before he answered. ''There was . . . I think there was an article about our tour. In one of the Austin newspapers. And I suppose that story could have been picked up and reprinted in other papers as well. That's common enough practice, isn't it?''

Longarm grunted. And wondered if there was any way the Austin paper would even know if its story was reprinted elsewhere. That was something he should ask. Get a wire off to Billy Vail's secretary Henry, perhaps. Henry was a whiz at finding out nit-picking details like that. ''So pretty much anybody could know where you'll be on a given day?''

16

"More or less," McWhortle said. "We've had to make some minor adjustments along the way, of course."

"Any o' those changes take place *before* these robberies occurred?" Longarm asked.

"I can't say right off the top of my head," McWhortle told him. "I suppose I could compare our current itinerary with the original and check them both against the dates of the robberies if you can give those to me," he suggested.

In point of fact, Longarm did not happen to have the specifics of the robberies. The information he'd received back in Denver had been incomplete. And Longarm hadn't thought to write down what little he was told. Billy expected McWhortle to have more firsthand knowledge than was the fact. At least that was certainly the impression Longarm got at the time. It looked like the telegraphic inquiry to Henry would have to grow somewhat longer.

"What about Billy's plan for me t' join the team? His idea was that it could be useful t' have somebody traveling on the inside o' things, so to speak," Longarm said. And added, "But not as a pitcher, o' course.

"I already told the boys we were expecting a new pitching prospect," McWhortle said. "Let me think. . . ." He smiled. "I believe we can make it work anyway."

Longarm raised an eyebrow.

"You are still an ace pitcher from Denver," the ball club manager said, "but you hurt your shoulder. You can't pitch until it heals, but in the meantime you can stick with the team and travel along with us. In fact, we'll play you a little. Can you catch a ball?"

"You don't mean like one o' those fellas that crouches down behind the batter and gets his face mashed in a couple times every game? I don't wanta sound like a sissyboy, McWhortle, but those guys must be as dumb as they are tough. And I ain't yet seen one of them with all his teeth

17

still in his head. If that's what you got in mind for me then thanks but no thanks."

The young man chuckled. "That isn't the kind of catching I had in mind. What I meant was, if there's a ball falling out of the air can you run under it and catch it before it hits the ground."

Longarm shrugged. "Sounds easy enough, don't it."

"Oh yes," McWhortle agreed with a perfectly straight face. "Nothing to it at all."

"Yeah, I expect I can do that."

"Then while we wait for your shoulder to heal, Mr. Colorado Pitcher, we'll play you as a relief outfielder. A right fielder."

"Why that spot in particular?" Longarm asked.

"Because about the only balls ever hit into right field are struck by left-handed batters. And there are damn few of those on these small-time local clubs. It would be different against other professional clubs, of course. They make it a point to have left-handed batters so as to increase the odds of getting hits successfully. But on small amateur clubs," he shrugged, "a right fielder in games like these can go a week or more without ever having to actually catch a ball."

"That sounds pretty good t' me," Longarm admitted.

"How about your batting?"

Longarm grinned. "I dunno if I can hit a ball with one of your sticks, but if you throw the little sonuvabitch up in the air I can shoot it at least once before it hits the ground, maybe a couple times."

"Good of you to offer," McWhortle said in a dry tone, "but I'll have to check the rule book before I let you do that."

"Yeah, let me know what you find out."

"In the meantime we'll stick with the old-fashioned methods."

"Did you happen t' tell your fellows the name of this

18

player you was expecting from Denver?'' Longarm asked. ''Why?''

''I don't mean t' sound immodest, but if this bunch o' thieves are professionals, which it looks like they might be t' have things worked out so far ahead o' time, then there's a good chance they will've heard of a federal deputy named Long.''

''I see. If it makes you feel any better, I didn't know your name to tell to anyone. All Mr. Barnes said to me was that I could expect someone. He never said who.''

Longarm had the fleeting thought that maybe that damned Billy Vail had snookered him. Maybe the boss would have caved in had Longarm absolutely demanded the Leadville assignment. Maybe, dammit, Maeternick would have been saddled with this deal after all if Longarm had simply dug his heels in hard enough. Maybe that was why no name had been transmitted ahead of time.

Not that there was any point in thinking about that now. Dammit.

And not that Longarm could help but think about it at least a little bit. Dammit.

''I'd as soon fly false colors if you don't mind then,'' Longarm suggested out loud.

''It makes no difference to me. Just tell me who you are,'' McWhortle said.

Longarm pulled at his chin and gave a close examination to the soggy end of his cheroot. ''My mama once told me she'd thought of naming me Chester.'' He thought of something else and barked out an abbreviated laugh. ''My name is Long so I never before been called Short. So how's that for a new name? I'll be Chester Short, one first-class baseball pitcher from good ol' Denver, Colorado, Ewe Ess of Ay.''

McWhortle stuck his hand out for a shake. ''A pleasure to make your acquaintance, Chester Short. I certainly hope your shoulder gets to feeling better soon.''

"Yeah, thanks," Longarm said.

"We'll fix you up with a uniform this evening when we get back to the boardinghouse from practice. In the meantime you can have the rest of the day off. Tomorrow you'll begin working out the same as any other team member."

Longarm nodded and watched the manager head back to supervise the practice.

There was, Longarm—or rather Chet Short—reflected as he watched the players at work, quite a lot about the game of baseball that he did not know.

Yet.

Chapter 6

Before becoming a sure-enough baseball player, flannel uniform and all, Longarm thought it might be a fair idea for him to act like a deputy marshal just a little while longer. When he left McWhortle and the other boys playing their game behind the church building, Longarm headed not for the boardinghouse but back downtown where he'd seen the local jail a while earlier.

It was a place he did not particularly want to visit while dressed up like the athletic equivalent of a circus clown. An Austin Capitals uniform would call all too much attention to him, he was sure.

The jail, imposing structure that it was, had room enough inside for one six-by-eight cell, one undersized desk, one chair, and probably the smallest potbelly stove Longarm ever saw—a damned well useless item at this time of year—on a floor so crowded there would be no room for a coal scuttle in winter. Likely the man on duty would have to carry in fuel for the stove one piece at a time. There wouldn't be space enough for it otherwise.

At the time of Longarm's arrival the jail cell was occupied by a scruffy looking fellow with a three-day growth of beard, yellow teeth, and galluses holding up a pair of britches that were at least three sizes too big for him. The man—someone coming off a drunk, Longarm figured— was stretched out on the bottom of a pair of double-decker bunks and appeared to be sleeping. The ''office'' portion of the jail was empty.

Longarm stepped inside, looked quickly around—it didn't take long—and started to back out.

"Something I can do for you, mister?"

The fellow in the cell hadn't moved but his eyes were open, albeit barely.

"Sorry if I woke you," Longarm said.

"I was already awake, thanks."

"Yeah, well, I'm looking for the town marshal. Or police chief. Whatever you call him here."

"Grand Exalted Ruler of All He Surveys would be nice, I think," the fellow on the bunk said, still motionless and without any hint of a smile.

"Don't like your marshal much, huh?" Longarm observed aloud.

"Actually I'm real fond of the SOB," the man in the cell replied.

"You don't sound it."

"I'm allowed certain liberties in that regard."

"You the town drunk?" Longarm asked.

The man grinned and sat up on the side of the bunk. "Nope. Town marshal." He stood and pushed the cell door open. It hadn't been locked. "More comfortable taking siesta in here than out there, that's all. My name is Gene Darry. What can I do for you, mister?"

Longarm chuckled and introduced himself.

"Sure, you're the one they call Longarm, aren't you?" Darry said. "Out of Denver?"

"That's right."

"No offense, but I never heard of you," Darry said as he extended a hand to shake. He said it so deadpan and level that it took Longarm a second or two for it to sink in. Then he began to laugh. He thought he just might like Marshal Darry. Of course it remained to be seen if the fellow was any kind of lawman. Or if he needed to be.

"Now," Darry said, his voice crisp and businesslike for the first time, "what is it I can do for you, deputy?"

22

Chapter 7

"Look," Longarm said when he and Darry were done making plans for the day of the ball game, "I'd appreciate it if you wouldn't say anything 'bout this to anybody else. In particular I don't want anybody connected with the ball club t' know about it."

"What about the team manager?" the marshal asked. "You said he is helping you. Surely he's in the know."

"Not even him," Longarm confirmed.

"I don't understand. The man is a friend of your boss and is taking you onto the team. Surely you trust him."

Longarm shrugged. "I trust everybody, Gene. Up to a point. The thing is, this young fella is the son in law of a good friend o' my boss. That's a thin soup the way I see it. I mean, good girls been known to marry bad men from time t' time. And good men been known to make bad judgments when there's friendships an' kinships involved.

"Not that I suspect Douglas McWhortle. I sure as hell don't. But it occurs t' me that as long as I'm off someplace with that baseball team, I ain't gonna be where the action is. Which will be at a bank or post office or some such place in the town where the games are being played. So a smart thief, once he found out there was gonna be a lawman close by, would want to make sure that lawman was where he could be seen an' accounted for. You know?"

"That makes sense," Darry agreed.

"Which is why I'd rather you never said anything except to the boys you're putting on watch that day. An' not to

23

them until the last minute if it's all the same to you."

The town marshal nodded.

"As for McWhortle, I truly don't suspect him of being anything but the nice young fella he seems. On t'other hand, I don't figure to take any chances that aren't downright necessary."

"Sounds reasonable to me, Longarm. I'll keep shut about it. Even to the boys on your ball club." Darry smiled. "By the way, you got any suggestions which way a man should place his money come Saturday?"

"What happens Saturday?" Longarm asked.

Darry gave him an odd look. "That's the day they'll play the ball game, of course."

"Oh. Nobody mentioned that to me before. As for who you oughta bet on, that prob'ly depends on do you want t' lay your money down for politics or for profit."

Darry lifted an eyebrow and Longarm added, "Bet the home team if you want folks around town t' know you're supporting your own. But bet the visitors if you want t' pick up some easy cash. I seen the newspaper accounts o' this road trip, and they don't lose very many."

"Thanks."

"Mind telling me which way you'll play it?" Longarm asked. "Not that I got any right t' know, but I'm a mite curious."

Darry grinned. "Hell, that's easy. I'll lay ten dollars on the home team with Barney Pruitt. He's our town barber and never learned to keep a secret. But I'll put another twenty on the visitors and lay that one with Johnny Truaxe. Johnny is a saloon keeper and, well, has a few other business interests too that a law officer has reason to keep an eye on. Johnny runs a square game and knows how to stay shut about the things that matter."

Longarm smiled and stood, reaching for his hat. "Gene, it's been a pleasure meeting you. I'd enjoy spending more time with you, but I think it's best if we aren't seen together after this. I'll keep an eye on things from the ball field end of it and trust you t' have things under control back here in town come Saturday morning.''

''Afternoon,'' Darry corrected.

''Whatever.''

The two shook hands and Longarm ambled out into the afternoon sunshine. He supposed it would be some time before he would be free to do as he pleased again and likely he should enjoy a cool beer and maybe a steak before he joined up with the Austin Capitals.

He headed in the direction of the nearest of the several gentlemen's establishments in downtown Medicine Lodge.

Chapter 8

Longarm laid his cards down, a full house tens over fives. It should have been enough. It wasn't. "Beats me," he said as the young dirt farmer across the table showed four treys and a grin. The farmer was still grinning as he raked in the pot. Longarm figured the fourteen or so dollars of winnings would keep the kid and his family, if any, going for a month or better if he was sensible enough to hang on to it. Thinking about it that way made it a little easier to swallow the loss, most of which happened to be his since the others at the table had dropped out early in the deal.

"Gonna take your winnings back t' the wife now?" Longarm asked the boy, intending it to be more by way of suggestion than question.

"Quit when I'm hot? You'd like that, wouldn't you," the youngster returned.

Longarm shrugged. And pitched a ten-cent ante into the middle of the table.

"Two pair, jacks and nines," Longarm said. The kid across the way scowled and slammed his cards down. He'd only drawn two, but for the last half dozen or so hands he'd been becoming increasingly desperate to recoup his losses and Longarm had been pretty sure the boy was bluffing in the hope someone would actually believe he had three of a kind. No one had.

Longarm pulled in the pot—six dollars or a little more,

which must have looked pretty big to the kid by now—and anted up for the next deal.

"Draw poker, nothing fancy," said the man at his right whose turn it was to deal. "Ben, you're light."

The farmer didn't have much more than ten cents remaining in front of him. He picked through the meager pile of very small change until he had ten pennies separated from the herd and pushed them forward.

The man with the cards shuffled quickly and offered the deck to his right for a cut, then swiftly dealt out hands to each of the five players.

Longarm could see plain as a wart on a hog's nose that the farmer hadn't gotten shit in the deal. Likely not so much as a pair to build on. Longarm took his time picking up his own cards and looking them over—careful to *not* sort them when he did so—then fingering a quarter out of his own coin pile.

He hesitated a moment, then dragged the quarter back and pushed forward a nickel instead. "Open," he said. He probably should have gone for more, and would have, except that would buy the kid out of the game and Longarm didn't want to do that. Unlikely as it might be that the youngster could win again, if he insisted on being a damn fool then Longarm figured he deserved his shot.

And hell, lightning sometimes does strike twice.

Either the other players had nothing or they too wanted to go light so the kid named Ben could have a chance. Each of them called. As did Ben.

"Cards?" the dealer asked.

"I'm pat," Longarm said and placed his fanfold of cards facedown in front of him.

The rest of the gents each drew two except for the kid who tossed down three cards. It was all Longarm could do to keep from groaning out loud. Not even this boy Ben would be stupid enough to try another bluff for three of a kind. Which meant he was drawing two cards either to

27

make a flush—damned unlikely for that to happen—or even worse was trying to draw two to fill a straight.

There are times, Longarm reflected, when that kind of stubbornness stops being a display of *cojones* and becomes just plain stupid. This seemed like one of those times.

"Opener?" the dealer asked. "Your bet."

Longarm glanced over at the coins lying in front of the kid. There weren't so many of them that it was hard to count. "Eighteen cents," he said, pushing out two dimes and dragging back two of the pennies Ben had put in earlier. Longarm could have bet anything from nineteen cents up and taken the kid's chance away, but he didn't want to do that.

"Call," the next man said.

No one offered a raise, everyone seeming willing to go along and give Ben his last opportunity to recoup at least the price of a plug of tobacco and a beer.

"Everyone in?" the dealer asked unnecessarily. "That's fine then. Lay 'em down, gentlemen. Lay 'em down and we'll all weep but one of us."

The man to Longarm's left had a pair of jacks, the next man two kings and the dealer nothing stronger than a pair of treys.

Ben showed a pair of queens, but four of his cards were hearts. Obviously he'd been drawing two for the flush and paired up by sheer dumb luck. But not quite enough of it.

"Straight," Longarm said, laying his cards down for all to see. "Six high." Almost reluctantly he scooped the pot in.

"You cheating son of a bitch," Ben snarled.

"You talking to me, son, or to the man who dealt the cards?" Longarm asked mildly.

"You know who I mean, damn you," Ben spat back at him, pushing away from the table and pumping his right hand into a fist four or five times in rapid succession. He was not wearing a holster gun but there was a lump in the

28

right front pocket of his overalls that could have been a revolver.

"I expect I do at that, sonny. Fact is, you're wrong. I just hope you don't insist on being dead wrong."

"You cheated me! You . . ."

"Son, you'd best be careful how you use words like that. Say them to the wrong fellow and they can wind up caught in your throat, y'know?"

"I say you cheated, damn you," Ben cried loudly. He sprang to his feet angrily. Behind him, the room full of tipplers and friendly card players scrambled to get out of the way.

Longarm was leaning back in his chair with his hands laced lightly across his belly. With his left hand he casually pulled his coat open to show the butt of the big Colt lying only a few inches away from his hand.

"I don't want t' hurt you, boy. Go home now, and next time don't insist on bein' stupid."

"I say . . . I say . . ." The boy's mouth gapped and closed, gapped and closed. He was sucking air like a trout in a creel. He was scared. Longarm could see the fear stark in his eyes. He'd gone too far now. The problem was that he didn't know how to back water and get out of the situation he'd gone and created himself.

Somebody needed to give the kid an out, and it looked like there wasn't anyone else around who knew how to do it either.

Longarm reached out with his left hand, slowly, and picked up an empty shot glass the man to his left had been using. "Here," he said softly. He tossed the glass to the kid. Amber liquor sprayed high into the air. So, maybe the glass hadn't been empty after all.

Ben looked startled and, out of automatic reflex, moved to catch the glass. He blinked and stared into it.

When he looked up again he stared all the harder. But this time into the gaping muzzle of Longarm's .45. No one

29

in the place, including Ben, had so much as seen Longarm's hand move. One moment he was sitting leaned back in his chair. The next instant his posture was unchanged but now there was a dark and menacing double-action Colt in his fist.

If he needed an excuse to walk away, he damn sure had one now, Longarm figured.

"If it makes any difference to you," Longarm said gently, "I never cheated you. Didn't have to. Now go home, boy. Stop at the bar and have a drink if you like. Tell them I'm good for it. Then go home and tell your wife what you done with your seed money, or whatever it was you pissed away tonight. You hear me, boy? Go home."

The kid gulped hard. His eyes hadn't left the muzzle of the .45 since Longarm first showed it to him.

After several seconds of agonized indecision common sense finally broke through the irrational fog of his misery, and Ben turned and walked out into the night. He was still holding the small glass Longarm threw to him but did not stop to collect the offered drink.

"Jesus," someone nearby muttered.

Longarm sighed, then reached out and pulled the cards into a pile. "My deal, I believe," he observed to no one in particular.

Chapter 9

Longarm felt . . . silly. Dumb. On display. He suspected he now knew what it would feel like to show up for the party wearing a clown suit only to discover too late that it wasn't a masquerade ball after all but a formal sit-down dinner.

That is pretty much what it felt like to him to be out on the street in public, in broad daylight, wearing a tight—and damnably hot—flannel baseball costume.

He'd have covered the thing over with a duster or a slicker except the heat would've melted him into a puddle of rancid sweat before he got halfway to the playing field. As it was he was forced to walk the whole distance with people staring at him every step of the way, never mind that there were more than a dozen other idiots dressed in equally stupid uniforms walking alongside him. Every eye was on him and him alone. He believed that. And he really did somewhere at gut level even if he knew better in his conscious mind. He really did feel like a showoff asshole wearing what he personally regarded as children's clothes out where the grown-ups could see.

It was all part of the job though so the best he could do was grit his teeth and go along with it.

He dropped back in the pack to where the coach, who for some reason was called the manager and not coach, was speaking with the equipment boy, a kid with a club foot named Jerry something-or-other.

"Mr. McWhortle?"

"Douglas," the manager corrected. "What is it, Short?"

31

For a moment Longarm couldn't figure out where the short thing came in. Then he remembered that it was supposed to be his name here. He really was not feeling himself today. Likely, he guessed, the damn heat had cooked his brains and he would be useless ever after.

"Well?" McWhortle prodded.

"Oh, yeah. Now I remember. Why is it we had t' wait until afternoon to go out and do this practice stuff? I mean, why couldn't we do it in the morning before it got so stinking hot?"

McWhortle grunted and said, "Get used to it. The home team always uses the field in the mornings, wherever we go. For exactly the reason you bring up. It's more comfortable. That is, unless the weather pattern is rain in the mornings and sun in the afternoons. Then we'd have the honor of first practice."

"There's no room on one field for two clubs?" Longarm asked.

"Not for practices," McWhortle said, "unless you want fistfights and broken heads before the games. It's best to keep the locals and visitors apart. Count on it. Now if you'd excuse me . . . ?"

Longarm increased his stride, leaving McWhortle in deep conversation with Jerry, who was hopping along for all he was worth in the effort to keep up.

Off to the left in the shade of a front porch there was a gaggle of young women sitting in rocking chairs with a pitcher of what looked like lemonade between them.

They stopped rocking and leaned forward, hiding their mouths behind their hands but twittering like so many sparrows while the ball players walked by.

Longarm knew good and well those girls would be commenting about how stupid grown men looked when they were dressed up like idiots. How stupid and how very much out of place. He was sure of it, and he could feel his ears commence to burn as he hurried on down the street among his new "team mates."

He wished to hell he could get this over with.

Soon!

Chapter 10

"I got it. I got it." Longarm ran left, backpedaled two steps, moved left again shielding his eyes against the glare of the sun, inched forward a bit, left again, stuck his padded leather glove out in front of him . . . and felt the lousy little SOB of a ball tick the tips of his fingers on its way to thump onto the ground at his feet.

"Shit," he grumbled with a stamp of his boot—which was something he was going to have to take care of first chance he got as he'd not thought to pack shoes to bring along on the trip—and a grimace.

"Jesus, Short, just how stupid are you? Pick the ball up and throw it, the runner's still running."

Longarm remembered then. They were only practicing but supposed to be pretending it was like real. He looked around until he found the ball, picked it up and flung it toward the nearest Caps player.

"No, Short, not to the first baseman. The runner's already rounding second. You're supposed to throw to the cutoff man."

"Who the hell is that?"

"The second . . . never mind what he's called. That one. That guy standing there." The center fielder pointed.

"Him. Right. Thanks."

The center fielder gave him a decidedly ugly look, and Longarm thought most of the others were, too. Fortunately they were too far away to see clearly. Especially if a man didn't really *want* to see all that clearly.

"Sorry," Longarm mumbled but not so loudly that anyone else could hear.

"Man, I hope to hell you're as good a pitcher as Douglas was told you are."

"Soon as this shoulder gets t' feeling better you'll see for yourself," Longarm responded, silently adding, which won't be in your lifetime nor mine, ol' son.

The man, a third baseman named Esau, took a deep drink of water and wiped his mouth, then tossed the towel to Jerry. Esau shook his head. "I swear, Short, you play like you never saw this game before. You *have* seen a damn game before today, haven't you?"

"Three of 'em," Longarm said with a deadpan expression and hint of sarcasm in his voice. He was, however, telling the literal truth.

The players quickly drank up, toweled off, and trotted back out into the heat for more punishment.

Longarm dragged along behind them with all the enthusiasm of a man on his way to a dentist's chair.

"No, no, no, no, NO!!!"

Longarm blinked. Looked. Wondered what the hell he'd done wrong. This time.

He didn't have a clue. Not the first wee inkling.

But he knew he'd screwed up. Again. Oh, he was real sure of that.

He could tell by the way everybody else was glaring at him.

He sighed. And went into a crouch waiting for the guy with the stick to hit the ball again.

"Jeez, Short, catch the ball, will ya? Don't just *stand* there!"

"Catch . . . the ball," Longarm wheezed. "Yes, sir. First

thing. Catch the ball. I will . . . most definitely . . . keep that in mind. Sir.''

He considered keeling over sideways just for the relief of being able to lie down. Except he would still be in the stinking sun. God, it was hot. There wasn't a dry patch on him anyplace, not skin nor cloth nor the roots of his hair. He was drenched from one end to the aching other, and he was beginning to believe that this was a never-ending form of torture. He'd been deluded, that's what it was. He wasn't really on assignment in Kansas. The truth was that he'd died and been sentenced to perdition. And this right here was for damn sure it.

''Break time. Break, everybody. There's lemonade and sweet buns courtesy of the ladies over there, but everybody mind your language. We don't wanta shock anyone. Fifteen minutes, boys, then we'll take batting practice. Short, you'll be in the outfield running down balls and throwing them back in. You need the practice.''

''Yes, sir. Whatever you say, sir.'' *Running* down balls. Jesus. That was all he needed now. ''I hope you'll let me take some, uh''—he had to think hard for a moment to recall the term McWhortle had used—''batting practice too.'' He grinned, pretending to give a shit. The truth was that the fellow with the stick got to stand in one place, and that sounded pretty fine to Longarm right then. It would beat hell out of chasing balls and throwing them back anyway. Almost anything would. Longarm grinned and bobbed his head and tried to look just eager as all hell to take that practice at bat.

Chapter 11

"All right, children, that's enough for today. Let's get everything picked up and . . . no, wait a minute. Short. I promised you some batting practice, didn't I?"

Longarm hadn't intended to remind the manager of said promise. The idea to begin with was to find a soft job that would let him stand still for a little while. After several hours of loping back and forth across a grassy field in full sunshine and no shade, he was damn well ready to go back to the boardinghouse, soak in a tub of cool water until midnight, and then sleep right on through until time for the next practice session come tomorrow afternoon. That program or something mighty close to it. The idea of stopping for still more of this baseball bullshit was not really what Longarm had in mind at the moment.

McWhortle missed the point entirely, assigning a pitcher—a kid who needed extra work, obviously—and a couple ball chasers both in front of the bat and behind it.

McWhortle came over to Longarm and in a soft voice that the others wouldn't hear told him, "I'll have them throw you a few soft ones so you can get the feel of swinging the bat. Look, you, um, do know how to hold the bat and swing and all that stuff, right?"

"I been paying attention this afternoon. It looks easy enough," Longarm said.

"Don't count on it," the manager warned. Then, in a louder voice, said, "All right, everybody. The new man gets a few swings and we go in for supper."

Longarm picked up the nearest of several bats piled in the equipment cart and looked it over. The wood was pale and fairly nicely turned. Hickory, he guessed, or maybe ash. Not that he gave a damn. He waggled the thing like he'd seen some of the players do earlier in the day, then swished it back and forth through the air a few times for good measure. It felt to him pretty much like any good, stout stick ought to. The sort of thing a body might pick up to mash a rodent in the henhouse with, and surely it would be easier to hit a ball than a varmint. Anyway, Longarm's primary interest at the moment was to get this misery over with so he could get out of the afternoon sun.

"All right?" the pitcher, a kid named Dennis, called to him.

"Any time, I reckon." Longarm stood beside the piece of cloth they were using to mark home plate and lifted the bat off his shoulder.

The pitcher gave the ball a gentle toss, and Longarm whacked it as it came across the plate. The ball went over the head of the second baseman, a man named Watt, old enough he should've been out of short pants and kids' games, and somebody tossed the pitcher another ball to throw while Watt was off running down the first one.

Crack!

The ball flew high, caught the wind, and curved gently left before coming down well beyond the reach of the center fielder.

"Jesus Christ, Short, you haven't missed one yet," a voice blurted.

Longarm didn't see what was so remarkable about that, actually.

It wasn't like he was doing anything difficult. Shit, all he had to do was whack the ball with any part of the stick. And there never had been anything slow about his hands or anything wrong with his eyesight. Or his judgment. The simple fact that he was still alive was testament enough to that.

Why, compared with palming a gun and getting off half a dozen quick, loosely aimed shots, this was nothing at all.

And the truth was that he really could have shot the ball in midair.

Hitting it with a stick was nothing compared with that. Mere hand and eye coordination, that was all. Surely anybody could do it just easy as pie.

McWhortle motioned Dennis off the pitching mound, and Longarm relaxed. Good. They could go in now and cool off. Change out of these sweaty flannel uniforms and put on something decent. And dry.

He could practically taste that first beer. And this morning Mrs. Finney said there'd be chicken and dumplings for supper. Longarm couldn't remember the last time he'd had homemade chicken and dumplings. Now if McWhortle would just let them quit this nonsense and go back to the boardinghouse. . . .

"We're going to try something, Short. Jason, take Dennis's place out there. And, Jason . . ."

"Yeah, Doug?"

"Give Short your best stuff. No fooling around about it. Show him how the big boys play."

Jason, who was the ace pitcher on the club and who showed it in the cocky, almost contemptuous way he treated every other player on the squad, gave Longarm a wicked grin and swaggered out onto the mound.

The man stretched and grunted and kicked his leg high in the air.

When he heaved the ball it came so fast Longarm could actually hear its passage through the air. The baseball made a soft, sibilant, sighing hiss as it sped through the air and into the catcher's leather mitt.

Longarm swung at the thing but was too slow. The end of the bat came around after the ball was already by.

"See there, boy? That's the real thing," Jason crowed.

Longarm shrugged. It didn't make any difference to him whether he hit the stupid ball or not. "I think I see now, thanks. Try it again."

Jason reared back and let another one rip.

Longarm had it down this time. It was still nothing but a simple matter of making his hands go where his eye said they ought. But quicker this time. No big deal.

He connected so hard he could feel the sting of it through his palms and all the way into his wrists. The sound of the horsehide coming off wood was crisp and loud, and all around him the ball players began to gape as the ball soared damn near out of sight and then arced down toward the far end of the field.

The redhead center fielder, a skinny kid named Ted, didn't even try to run it down. He just stood there watching the thing sail over his head way the hell out of reach.

"That's a home run, Short. Jesus. I never seen anything fly so far."

That was good, Longarm thought. Wasn't it? He knew better than to ask though. Not right now. He could talk to McWhortle about it later if he remembered. He settled for turning his head and spitting, which seemed to be something the other players did a lot. "Can we quit now?"

"Good God, no," McWhortle said. The young manager looked so tickled about something that he could bust although Longarm didn't know what had happened to please him so. "Come on, Jason. Put something past Short here. If you can."

Longarm shrugged and picked up the bat again. Now if they could just go ahead and get this over with. . . .

Chapter 12

Longarm had never in his life been so tired, so hot, or so thoroughly drenched with steamy-sticky sweat. He was sure of it. Except maybe that time . . . no, not even then, he decided upon further reflection. This was the worst of it right here and now, yes it was.

His ass was dragging and his clothes—what asshole was it who decided that baseball uniforms had to be made of flannel, anyhow—stuck to him like they'd been painted on.

The other boys were fifteen to twenty yards in front of him and chattering like a flock of damn guinea fowl as they walked back to the boardinghouse. Even the club-footed equipment boy was moving along faster than Longarm, pushcart full of bats and all. Longarm might have been able to work up some humiliation over that fact except that it would've been too much effort. Right now all he wanted was a bath, a cool one at that, and about twenty hours of sleep. He was too tired even to want any supper. Or so much as a beer. And that, b'damn, was tired indeed.

"Yoo hoo. Mister. Mr. Short, is it? Chester Short?"

He squinted one eye against the sting of salty sweat that was streaming off his scalp and looked to see who was speaking to him.

She was eighteen, nineteen years old and built like a sword blade, lean and flexible. But pretty. Lordy, she was pretty. Chestnut hair done up in a prim and tidy bun, delicate face but full and rather juicy lips, eyes as icy pale as a she-wolf's. She looked good enough to eat. If a man

41

happened to be hungry, that is. At the moment Longarm was sure he was too tired to raise an erection if the girl had been naked. Which she certainly was not. She had that prissy, skinny-neck look about her that spoke of choirs and daylong sermons. He doubted a girl like this one would consent to get naked to take a bath. Likely she insisted on wearing a bathing robe to reach underneath and scrub.

Not that he cared, of course.

"Yoo hoo. Mr. Short?"

"Yeah." He slowed and came to a stumble-footed halt, not so much because he wanted to talk to the girl as that he wanted to rest for a minute before walking on to the boardinghouse and that waiting bathtub.

"I saw you hitting those home runs this afternoon. It was wonderful. Really." Her smile was beatific, and her eyelashes fluttered right furiously. "You were magnificent."

Longarm felt his cheeks commence to heat up. He wasn't exactly used to this sort of praise. It was positively embarrassing. Magnificent? Jeez!

"Could you come into the arbor here for a minute, please?"

"You want my autograph or something?" he asked. "Me?"

The smile became even more fetching. If that was possible.

"Please?" she repeated.

Damn girl had dimples when she smiled like that. And what man can resist the request of a pretty young thing with dimples? "Sure, why not."

Wearily Longarm trudged along behind the girl as she let herself through a white-painted gate and through the yard of a fine and fancy house to a spacious gazebo so thoroughly covered with ivy and climbing rose vines that it might as well have had walls. "In here," she said.

It was coming dusk—McWhortle hadn't wanted to quit

42

despite the late hour and only agreed to let Longarm stop batting when he complained that he couldn't see the ball any longer; a mild sort of lie but a necessary one considering the state of Longarm's fatigue—and inside the summerhouse it was practically full dark.

The girl stopped half a pace into the shelter and turned, her right hand reaching out—and down—to unerringly find the bulge that Longarm's pecker made high on the thigh of his wet uniform britches.

"Short," she said with a small laugh. "They should rename you Long. I couldn't believe it when I saw this lump, Chester. Why, I do believe it is as big and powerful as the bat you were swinging."

What Longarm couldn't believe was what this crazy girl was all of a sudden doing.

She pressed herself full against him, which surely did no good to the pretty dress she was wearing as it, and she herself, would be wallowing in his sweat from the merest touch.

She came up onto tiptoes and shoved her tongue inside his mouth, all the while pulling and tugging at his prick.

Longarm couldn't believe that. Nor could he quite believe his own reaction.

Tired though he undoubtedly was, damned if he wasn't getting hard.

The girl pulled back a mite and grinned. "You really are magnificent, Chester."

Longarm grunted. Hell, he didn't know what he properly should say under these circumstances, so a grunt would simply have to suffice.

"Magnificent," she murmured, the sound partially muffled against his chest as she dropped down onto the heels of her feet and began nuzzling his sweat drenched chest.

Before he knew what she was about she abandoned her hold on his pecker and started unfastening the buttons of his shirt. She spread the cloth wide and damned if she

43

didn't begin licking his chest, licking the sweat off him as greedy-happy as if it was chocolate syrup.

She ran her tongue over his chest and belly and then paid particular attention to his nipples, which proved to be just about fifteen or maybe twenty times as sensitive as he would've expected them to be.

The more she licked the harder his erection got and the wider the girl's grin as she reached down to fondle him some more.

After a couple minutes of that—he wouldn't have objected if she'd decided to camp out there and lick him until, say, daybreak—she began to droop lower and lower and lower still.

Her tongue ranged down across his belly, investigated the inside of his navel, and then explored new territory as her insistent fingers opened buttons to make way.

By then she'd surely drunk at least a pint of day-old sweat, but that sure didn't seem to bother her any.

She deftly slipped his cock free of the last restraints of clothing and, on her knees by now, began licking that too.

"Magnificent," she mumbled over and over as she licked and fondled and then began to suck right strenuously.

Longarm felt like she might accidentally suck his balls out of their pouch and pull them on through his pecker.

Which was not a complaint. No, ma'am, it was not. Merely an observation of passing interest.

The girl's pretty little head bobbed and darted like a woodpecker pecking wood while she sucked so hard it damn near hurt.

Damn near, that is.

He was not inclined to make her quit.

In an amazingly brief time he felt the sap commence to rise. The pressure increased until he couldn't hold it in any longer, and he turned a gusher loose inside the girl's mouth. He didn't actually time the explosion but his guess was that he pumped juice into her for something on the order of four or five minutes—well, that's what it *felt* like anyhow—before the well finally ran dry and the girl rocked back onto her heels with a broad, satisfied grin.

"I do so love that flavor, Chester," she said.

Longarm had no response for that.

Didn't need one anyway.

The girl tucked his limp dong back where she'd found it, buttoned his fly and then his shirt and got him all tucked in and presentable again, then without another word turned and disappeared through the far side of the gazebo.

It was dark out by then and Longarm could not see where she went from there.

He was halfway to the boardinghouse before he realized that he had no idea who the girl had been. She hadn't so much as given her name.

He thought on it some and decided he could forgive her the social faux pas.

Chapter 13

"Have a nice time, Chet?"

It took Longarm a few seconds to remember that he was the one being addressed, that these ball players knew him as Chester Short. As the last one to arrive at the table, he took the chair at the distant end, furthest from the platters of food, and pretended not to notice all the guffawing and chuckling that the others were doing.

"That Cherry," the first baseman said, "she could suck a walnut through a cattail reed, eh, Short?"

"I don't know what you're talking about," Longarm lied. Which only served to make the laughter all the louder.

The first baseman—Longarm didn't know his proper name; he was simply called Hoosier, which might or as easily might *not* mean he was from Indiana—made a vulgar gesture that set the rest of them off into gales of laughter.

"Did she tell you she's a virgin, Chet?" Watt asked. "Bet she did and you didn't believe her, right? Funny thing about it is that she wasn't lying. I felt her when it was my turn. Cherry's cherry is there all right, just like she claims. Little bitch will suck a man dry like one of those black spiders or she'll take it in the ass if you want, but she won't let nobody inside her snatch. Claims she's saving that for when she gets married. As if anybody'd be stupid enough to marry her."

"No point buying a cow when the milk's free, right?" Caleb put in.

Longarm was not particularly enjoying the dinner table

conversation. Especially considering the fact that the food was being served by a dark-skinned young girl, Mexican he guessed or half-breed Mexican and Negro, who tried hard to pretend she didn't hear but whose embarrassment was given away by the flush of deep red that darkened her ears and gave her cheeks a glow.

For that matter it didn't please him a whole hell of a lot to discover that, or so it seemed, he was the last man on the team to receive the amorous attentions of the girl called Cherry. Judging from the talk at the table everyone with the possible exceptions of Douglas McWhortle and the club-footed equipment boy had already had their times at bat. So to speak.

Longarm ate quickly. Which was pretty easy to do since by the time the plates and bowls and platters reached his end of the table there wasn't much left on them to slow a fellow down with excess chewing.

Fortunately he was still too tired to be hungry, even after a cool bath, so it didn't hurt his feelings much to be overlooked when it came to the groceries.

Quick as Longarm was to finish some of the other boys who'd started sooner got done even quicker; this was not a crowd to linger over coffee and pleasant chitchat. As soon as a plate was clean, its user was on his feet and away. Longarm ate what he could and then left the table.

On his way to the outhouse he took a shortcut through the kitchen to reach the back door but he stopped when he stepped through the connecting door from the dining room only to find one of his teammates standing half in and half out the back door, whispering fast and furious to someone Longarm couldn't see in the shadows on the back porch.

Longarm saw the left field slugger named Nat when the guy turned his face in response to the motion of Longarm's arrival and shut his mouth in a big hurry when he saw he wasn't alone in the kitchen. Longarm wasn't positive but he thought Nat waved the guy outside away, gesturing with one hand that was partially hidden by his body.

The person on the porch shook his—or her, Longarm couldn't see for sure—head and looked like he/she wanted to protest the dismissal, but Nat scowled and reached out the door to give the person a slight shove.

Before Longarm could get a look at who was out there, the shadows moved. And became empty.

Whoever Nat was talking with was gone.

And damned curious behavior it was, Longarm thought.

Dumb bastards. Longarm wouldn't have thought a thing about the incident if the guy on the porch had come inside so the two parties could stand there in the lamplight and talk over whatever it was they wanted to discuss.

But this . . . this seemed damned suspicious.

Was Nat connected with the robbers? Giving them information about the team movements? Or whatever?

At the moment Longarm had no answers to those questions nor to very many others.

But he was sure of one thing. From now on he intended to keep a particularly sharp eye on young Nat the slugger in the opposite field.

Chapter 14

The dawning of game day found Longarm—he could hardly believe it—downright apprehensive.

It wasn't like this was anything of genuine importance, for crying out loud. But there it was anyway. His gut had that twisting, turning, churning sensation in it, and the more he thought about standing out in the middle of a ball field with maybe several hundred people peering at him the more nervous he became about the whole thing.

He would rather be in a gunfight than . . . well, almost rather. At least that was something he was familiar with, something he'd done before.

This baseball shit was something else again.

But then with any kind of luck McWhortle wouldn't go so far as to send him out in front of everybody. After all, it was pretty well established by now that Longarm couldn't catch a batted ball for sour apples.

The team slept in late and was served a huge breakfast. "Remember to pack your bags and bring them downstairs when you're called to go to the field," the manager told everyone while he had them at the table. "Jerry will have a cart out front ready for you to load everything onto. We'll be going straight from the ball field to the train station, won't be back here again, so don't leave anything behind."

Longarm wasn't sure if the reminders were mostly for his sake as a newcomer or if McWhortle went through this same spiel at every stop.

"Get some rest now. I'll call you down about eleven.

The game is at one o'clock sharp. Any questions? Any problems?''

No one said anything and after a few moments the manager released them with a wave of his hand. Longarm hung back behind the others. He wandered over to McWhortle and asked, "Is there anything special I need t' watch out for?"

"Not that I know of," McWhortle admitted. Then the man grinned. "Are you ready to play some ball today, Mr. Short?"

Longarm rolled his eyes. Then went upstairs and stretched out on his bed to catch a few spare winks while he had the chance.

Longarm yawned and by habit reached for an inside coat pocket in search of a cheroot. Except of course he wasn't wearing a coat and there was no place in or on a baseball uniform suitable for carrying fragile cigars. Dammit.

Out on the field things were going just fine for the visiting team. In the sixth inning the Capitals were up on the locals by a score of 11 to 3, and by now Longarm was familiar enough with the team's play to realize that the boys from Texas were loafing.

A chubby, yellow-haired man who should have been old enough to know better than to mess in kids' games was up to bat for the home team. The Caps' pitcher, the one named Dennis something-or-other, sent one in low and hard and the fat boy bashed it. The ball dribbled across the infield to the second baseman Watt who scooped it up and held it several long seconds before he tossed it on to Hoosier, the first baseman.

Watt timed his throw to arrive about half a heartbeat ahead of the charging, puffing fat man. Hoosier caught the ball, putting the batter out, but he wasn't satisfied with that. The batter was already committed in a hard run and didn't have time to pull up if he tried. Hoosier could have stepped out of the way and let the fat guy run on by, but he didn't. Instead he dropped his shoulder and braced himself, and the much older and softer local slammed into him like a berserk rooster running full tilt into a barn wall.

There was a cloud of dust and some serious squealing and the fat blond fellow wound up rolling around on the ground clutching himself like he'd been kneed in the nuts. And hell, maybe he had. Longarm hadn't particularly noticed amid all the other activity.

There were screams of protest from the crowd—five hundred folks or more, Longarm calculated when he looked them over—and the local team's manager came running out to protest to the umpire.

McWhortle came out to protest the other team's protest, and for a while it was all shouts and curses and loud accusations.

Longarm thought the visiting crowd was finding it all pretty funny. And apparently pretty normal, too.

No one, not even his own manager, was paying much attention to the fat guy and after a bit he dragged himself to his feet and stumbled back to the home team bench to try and get some air back into his lungs. He looked pale and on the verge of puking, Longarm thought, but the guy took it straight up and never joined into the complaining.

All in a day's fun, Longarm thought a trifle sourly. Or was this supposed to be work? He was never quite sure which was supposed to be which with these people.

"Jerry."

"Yes, Mr. Short?"

"Where's that cart, son? I need to go get a smoke."

The equipment boy told him where to find the cart with all their gear piled onto it, and Longarm got up, stretched hugely, and went off in the direction Jerry indicated.

Chapter 15

Longarm sucked the smoke deep into his lungs and held it there, savoring the taste of it for a moment before he reluctantly exhaled. There is nothing that can quite compare with the flavor of a good cigar. Or so he often claimed. At other moments, of course, he might find himself induced to consider certain other pleasures even finer. At the moment, however, it was a cheroot he had in hand and so at this moment it was the smoke that he found most enjoyable.

When finally he exhaled he did so onto his match, extinguishing the flame in the process. He snapped the spent matchstick in half and dropped it onto the ground beside the baggage cart, then took another deep drag on the cheroot before turning back in the direction of the playing field where the Austin Capitals were lazily destroying the local nine.

"You!"

It took Longarm a moment to remember who the idiot was.

"You son of a bitch," the boy accused.

"Still blaming me for your own stupidity, eh, sonny?" Ben. That was the kid's name, he recalled now. Lousy poker player and a hothead too. That was a pity, Longarm thought.

"You ain't carrying a gun to threaten me with this time," the poor loser crowed.

"It'll be a cold day in Hell before I need one to take care of a pup like you," Longarm told him.

"You son of a bitch."

"Try an' be a little original, will you? You used that one once already."

"Son of a bitch," the boy repeated.

"Leave it alone, son. You play poker badly enough without showing yourself off as a horse's ass too."

"You damn ball players. Come in here and strut around. Make fun of us. Cheat us and steal our money and our women too. I'm gonna teach you a lesson, mister. You and all them other sons of bitches too."

Longarm sighed. "I let you off easy the last time, sonny. You might not be s' lucky this time around. Now let it be while you still can. Take some good advice an' go home. All right?"

Damnfool kid still had that same lump in his pocket and the bulge still looked to Longarm like the sort of thing that would be caused by, say, a short-barreled hideout revolver. The dumb little SOB stuffed his hand into his pocket to go after the thing.

Longarm had no idea what the young imbecile thought his intended victim was supposed to do while he was fishing inside his overalls for the gun. Panic maybe or else faint away in a dead fright.

Neither of which Longarm was much inclined to do.

Longarm was carrying his derringer but didn't want to use it. After all, everybody is born stupid. The trick is to let them grow and learn long enough to get over that handicap. While Ben was groping inside his britches, Longarm stepped in close to him and clamped an iron grip around the wrist of the hand that was buried inside the pocket.

With his other hand Longarm bopped the kid—not even all that hard—briskly across the bridge of his nose.

Ben's eyes widened and his nose began to bleed like a major artery had been slashed wide open.

Which was the idea to begin with. Lots of fuss and fury to get the kid's attention but no real damage done.

Apparently, though, young Benjamin wasn't accustomed to seeing his own blood.

He looked down with horror at the scarlet stain spreading over his shirt and the grubby bib of his overalls.

And he screamed.

Not just a yelp. A real hog-sticker of a scream. A king sized, throat-ripping, mind-numbing, rip-roarer of a scream it was.

It damn sure was enough of a scream to command the attention of all the hundreds of people gathered around that field for the ball game.

And then as if to punctuate the grandeur of that fine scream, the idiot youngster compounded it with an involuntary squeeze of both hands . . . one of which happened to have hold of the little gun that was still in his pocket.

The gun went off with a sharp if somewhat subdued crack—the noise of it wasn't a patch on the quality of the scream that preceded it—and the kid shifted from a magnificent scream into a terrified wail that shuddered and shifted and ululated like a warbling buzzard gone mad.

Longarm glanced down and saw why. Now, in addition to the harmless flow of blood from the kid's battered nose, there was another and perhaps more sinister flow from high on his thigh. Damn youngster had gone and shot himself when he jerked off a shot inside his own pocket. Well, Ben hadn't yet shown cause why he should be awarded any medals for intelligence.

"Look, kid, if you'll be quiet for a minute we'll see can we find a doctor to. . . ."

"Murder! Murder! He's trying to kill me. *Help!*"

The little fucker was shouting that as loud as his first scream had been.

And as for attention . . . he sure as hell had it now.

Some of the rowdier elements among the crowd of baseball fans, many of them with the contents of pint bottles already safely stowed away inside their bellies, began to pay attention to the pleas of their beleaguered comrade.

One at a time, then quickly in pairs and trios and whole damn gobs, they came rushing to the rescue of a hometown boy who they saw as being assaulted and perhaps even shot at by some smartass out-of-town baseball professional from that team that was humiliating their own fine boys.

No doubt these fine young men thought it their civic duty to defend the honor and the person of this poor innocent who was being so foully abused by the bigger, taller, stronger stranger. And seeing their duty they rushed to do it, fists balled and throats quickly becoming hoarse from the fury of their shouts.

Oh, shit! Longarm thought.

He had just about time enough to form that thought.

Then the wave of enraged humanity reached him with all the impact of a storm wave crashing onto a rocky shore. And rolled right over him.

Chapter 16

Didn't these people ever *bathe*? Longarm's face was mashed tight against the belly of some farmer whose shirt smelled—tasted too for that matter—of assorted types of sweat including what Longarm guessed as being human, mule, milk cow, and with maybe a hint of goat thrown in for good measure.

It was uncomfortable as hell. On the other hand it could have been worse. The good thing was that there were so many of them, and they were piled so deep on top of him, that there wasn't room enough for any of them to get any decent punches landed. The dozen or so who'd swarmed over him just kind of wallowed around and got in each other's way while Longarm was buried at the bottom of the heap trying to get some breath into his aching lungs.

The guy on top of him shifted to one side and sort of slid off and next thing Longarm knew there was someone's hairy ear in his face. He bit it.

The aggrieved party howled in pain and raised up enough that Longarm could gulp some fresh air before the pile closed in again.

Above the din of disorganized combat that raged above and about him, Longarm could hear a new chorus of shouts and threats and whatnot.

He thought he recognized some of the voices. Was sure of it when bodies began flying off him. Soon he could see the Capitals, every one of them, including the undersized and presumably more-dignified-than-this manager, laying into the crowd of locals with fists, feet, and whatever else came to hand.

No bats though, Longarm noted as he scrambled to his feet. No bats. That was good. He ducked underneath a roundhouse swing thrown by a burly man in a black suit-coat and batwing collar and reacted to the fancy-dan with a left jab that would leave one proud-looking shiner before the next morning.

"Ouch," the man protested.

Longarm shrugged. And popped him one on the other eye. Might as well make it a matched pair.

Something slammed into Longarm's back square between the shoulder blades. He was driven to his knees, and he swiveled to meet his attacker and came up swinging. The blow caught the fellow in the gut and doubled him over, gasping for breath that just wouldn't come. Meanwhile the other man, the one with the twin soon-to-be black eyes, took careful aim with an entirely too solid right that rattled Longarm's teeth. Longarm grunted, spit out a little blood, and returned the favor by dropping the Kansas boy with a hard shot that caught him flush on the jaw and blew his lamp out slick as greased shot.

While this was going on, the rest of the Caps were having their own tussles. Men were shouting, bleeding, cursing, kicking, throwing and ducking punches, and in general having a fine old time of it.

The locals outnumbered the visitors from Texas, but as it had been with the now interrupted game, it appeared that it was the visiting team that had the edge in experience and ability if not necessarily in the area of willingness. The local boys were game but the simple truth was that they were outclassed.

Longarm saw the red-headed center fielder—Ted, was it? he thought so—snatch a man twice his size off the back of his outfield companion Nat and cut the big man down to size while Nat was busy breaking the nose of an unlucky

Kansan who didn't duck in time.

Caleb, the catcher, took a vicious-looking punch square in the face and hardly blinked—but then, hell, a mere punch would hardly compare with the punishment of catching a foul ball flush on the puss—before grabbing the offender by the belt and lifting him bodily overhead. With a roar Caleb threw the fellow at a trio of onrushing locals. All four, counting the one Caleb tossed, went down like so many duckpins and rolled around on the ground with arms and legs flying.

Things might've gone on like that for some time except some of Marshal Darry's whistle-blowing coppers came along and stopped the fun.

The local deputies took charge like they knew what they were doing. They both carried hickory batons and weren't shy about applying them—carefully though so as to inflict more than a mite of quick pain but not anywhere that would cause actual damage. They mostly went for the meaty parts of a man's thigh so he would feel the bruising for the next week or so but where nothing would be busted and no organs could be ruptured. Longarm admired the technique for the professionalism it showed.

"All right now, dammit, everybody be still and. . . ."

Ben, the young asshole who'd started all this, tried to pipe up with a mouthful of complaint which the older of the two deputies quickly snubbed short.

"You." The cop pointed his baton at Ben. "Shut your mouth or you'll be the first to look inside a jail cell."

"Yes, uh, sir." Ben was lying on the ground with blood all over him, clinging to his right leg with both hands where he'd shot himself.

"I don't want to hear a word. Not from any one of you until I ask. And then you'll talk to me one at a time. Do I make myself clear?" The policeman glared slowly around the now silent circle of combatants. "All right. Now I want you to separate. Ball players over there." He pointed. "Ev-

58

eryone else over here. And don't a single damn one of you say a word, not one, until I look you in the eyes and give you permission to speak. Are we clear? Is everybody happy? Fine. Now move. Nice and slow. That's it.''

Longarm shut his mouth, looked around on the ground for the cheroot he'd been enjoying when this mess got started—couldn't find it though, dammit—and moved to do as he was damn well told.

Chapter 17

The local lawmen were sensible enough to be more interested in peace than in retribution. They cut the visitors out
of the herd and sent them all packing after declaring the
lopsided ball game over and done with.

That was just fine by the ball players, most of whom by
that time were fairly well battered. They might have beat
hell out of the locals on the ball field, but prowess most
often has to bow to the sheer weight of numbers when it
comes to a brawl. And this time was no different. There
were more of the Kansans than there were Texas boys, and
that right there proved to be the long and the short of it
when bumps and bruises were handed out in the free-for-
all.

Longarm himself had a nasty gash in the vicinity of his
left eyebrow, a shoulder that would be sore as hell for the
next couple days, what felt like a bruised tailbone—either
from a fall or from being stomped on while he was already
down, he wasn't sure which—and knuckles that looked like
they'd been run across a cheese grater about five times too
many.

The other boys had similar assorted ailments.

But then so did a good many of the members of the mob
that jumped them.

All in all, Longarm thought, it could be said that a good
time was had by all.

And a fair time if you wanted to look at it that way. The
Capitals won on the field but the locals reclaimed their

honor in the melee that followed.

Longarm had lost track of the inept poker player who had started the whole thing. Which was all right, really. Longarm damn sure didn't want anything from the boy. And this way the affair ended without anybody being shot. There was much to be said for that.

Douglas McWhortle looked his players over after the coppers were done chewing on them. The team manager planted his hands on his hips and tried, probably for the benefit of any of the locals who might be paying attention, to sound like he actually cared that there had been a fight.

"All right, everybody, you heard what the officer said. Stay together in a bunch and go . . . quiet, mind . . . straight to the train station. Our train is scheduled to leave in—" McWhortle pulled a watch from his pocket and consulted it—"in a little less than an hour. I want you all to keep together. No stragglers and no stopping to bellyache with the hometown folks. Above all don't any of you try and sneak away for a drink. You hear me? I'll make sure you get something on the train, but don't get into any more trouble here in town. The police here aren't giving us a hard time about this, so let's not give them any more grief either. Nat, Esau, that goes for you two especially. It's over, and let's leave it that way. Jerry, is the cart all right?"

"Yes, sir. Nobody bothered it none."

"All right then. You're in charge of that. And keep an eye on this crowd, will you? If anybody tries to sneak off on his own. . . ."

"I'll tell you, boss. You know I will."

"You all heard that, I hope. Jerry will be watching you while I go by the box office and get our split of the receipts. Go on now. You all know the way. I'll meet you there in about a half hour."

While all that was going on, Gene Darry's deputies were giving the local crowd a talking to—with more than a few winks and grins, Longarm noted—to keep them out of trouble.

That was all just so much window-dressing, of course. The deputies would keep up an appearance of tough talk while making sure they didn't damage the pride of the home folks and while keeping the fun from escalating into something that could have been dangerous instead of the harmless amusement it actually turned out to be.

McWhortle hustled off in the direction of the ticket booth, and Jason Hubbard, the number one pitcher, more or less took charge of the ball players, shooing them away from the battleground and on toward the train station.

As they walked it occurred to Longarm that none of the ball players seemed to find it at all exceptional that every manjack among them should have come rushing to Longarm's defense once the punches started flying.

He sidled over to Dennis, number three or four among the pitchers and one of the youngest members of the Capitals, and asked the kid about it.

Dennis gave him a wide-eyed look of puzzlement and said, "Hell, you're a teammate, aren't you?" As if that explained everything.

And perhaps, Longarm thought, it really did. He was a stranger, true, but a Cap as long as he was wearing the uniform. Accustomed to working alone, and in a business where sportsmanship and cooperation were not exactly priority items, that was something he wasn't really used to. For these boys, though, maybe it really was that simple. A teammate was in trouble, so what else would they have done but jump into the fray right along with him.

He found that attitude to be amusing in a way. But kind of touching too.

He slapped Dennis lightly on the shoulder, then drifted back through the moving pack until he was beside the baggage cart. He was still hankering for a good smoke and hadn't had time to finish one in entirely too long.

Chapter 18

The manager was late getting back from whatever errands he'd been on. He barely made it to the station in time to shoo the team onto the train ahead of him. Longarm attributed McWhortle's grim expression to his concern for meeting the train schedule.

He was wrong.

"Bad news, boys," the manager said once they were all assembled in the smoking car.

"How'zat, boss?"

"There isn't any money to pay you with," McWhortle announced.

If the man was looking for dramatic effect, he damn sure found it. There was a disbelieving silence among the shocked ball players. And almost as quickly there was anger to follow the initial disbelief.

"What the hell d'you mean by that? We all seen the size of that crowd. There has to've been a good gate. More than enough."

"There was a good gate all right," McWhortle agreed, "but while that fight was going on some son of a bitch snuck into the ticket booth and stole the cash box."

"But . . ."

"I know. I know, dammit. The men in the booth should have been watching it, but they weren't. Once the fight started they both went running to see. They neither one of them gave a thought to the money though they should have. They realize that now that it's too late, of course."

63

"But what about our money? How can we get along without our pay?"

McWhortle didn't look a lick happier than the complaining team members. He scowled and shook his head. "I have enough left over from our earlier stops to make our expenses for another couple days. After that we should have the gate from the next game. We'll make it through. But there just isn't anything in the kitty to provide for pay. I'm sorry."

"What about the guarantee? Didn't we have a guarantee for the game today?"

"Sure we did. The local organizers said they don't owe it because the gate receipts were well above the minimum they guaranteed we'd draw. They say it isn't their fault that the gate was stolen. And of course it isn't. I told them we'd sue. They said that's fine and told me where I could file. They know good and well we can't afford the time or the money to do that." McWhortle sighed. "I guess it wasn't much of a bluff. I'm sorry. Really."

Most of the men looked disappointed, but only two or three looked all that put out by the loss.

Later Longarm asked the manager about the pay. It was something he hadn't considered before, not being a legitimate member of the club.

"We pay five dollars a game and found," McWhortle told him. "Expenses are higher than you might think and the gates are never all that big. So, as a team we don't make much in the way of a profit. Enough to cover what's necessary, usually. Not a whole lot over. This time . . ." He shrugged and shook his head.

"Tough," Longarm said.

"Tell me about it. Oh, I have something for you."

"For me?"

"I didn't want to give it to you until we were alone," McWhortle explained, digging into a pocket and coming up with a somewhat rumpled square of paper that had been folded and refolded. "From the sheriff back there."

Gene Darry wasn't the county sheriff but Longarm didn't bother trying to explain the difference between a sheriff and a town marshal or police chief. It was a distinction few civilians bothered to make.

"Thanks." He glanced around to make sure none of the other players was paying attention—they weren't; for the most part they were concentrating on the several bottles of cheap whiskey McWhortle had brought aboard with him as a consolation for not having their pay in hand—and unfolded the note, which proved to be pretty much what he expected.

NO ACTION IN TOWN DURING GAME. STAKEOUT CAME UP EMPTY. NO STRANGERS REPORTED TODAY EITHER. FIGURE TICKET BOOTH THEFT UNRELATED TO YOUR STRING OF ROBBERIES. SORRY. BETTER LUCK NEXT STOP. DARRY

Longarm grunted and folded the paper back along its original creases before stuffing it—or trying to—into a pocket.

Damned baseball uniform. For a little while there he'd forgotten he was wearing the silly thing.

"Excuse me," he said. "I'm gonna find my bag and change into something human."

"All our gear is back in the luggage car. Oh, come to think of it, poor Jerry doesn't know about the theft yet."

"You want me to tell him?" Longarm asked.

McWhortle shook his head. "He should hear it straight from me. Just ask him to come up here and see me."

"Can do." Longarm began moving back along the clattering, swaying string of Plains and Pacific R.R. cars. He would feel better once he was in his own clothing and had some cheroots and matches handy in his pockets, he was sure. Pockets. Damn. Helluva idea, pockets.

65

Chapter 19

There is a rule, surely written down somewhere and probably carved in granite, too, that requires all desired objects to be placed at the bottom of whatever pile is being searched. Longarm wasn't sure just who decreed that this be so, but he was pretty sure the rule existed somewhere, somehow.

And sure-damn enough, his carpetbag was smack on the bottom of the jumble of bags, boxes, duffels, and pokes belonging to the ball players.

"You want me to fetch it out for you, Mr. Short?" the equipment boy offered in a tone of voice that was half-hearted but nonetheless decent of him.

"No thanks, Jerry. Mr. McWhortle wants to talk t' you, and you wouldn't want t' keep him waiting."

The clubfooted kid looked relieved as he hurriedly made his way forward into the next car and out of Longarm's sight.

Longarm paused for a moment—but only for a moment; after all his cheroots were inside that bag—then began tugging and shoving at all the bundles so as to extricate his own gear from among all the rest.

Once he had it the first order of business was to find, quickly trim, and gratefully light a smoke. After that he pulled a decent set of clothing out. He hated having to wear the damned clown suit that the baseball players found to be so comfortable. Or seemed to. At least none of them seemed interested in changing clothes.

With proper clothing in hand he glanced around the baggage car with some small amount of concern. It was unlikely anyone would wander in while he was changing. But there were some ladies present in the passenger coaches forward and it was not inconceivable that one of them would choose to traipse along to the baggage car to replenish an empty perfume bottle . . . or to sneak a nip of Lydia Pinkham's mostly alcohol elixir.

Unlikely, sure. But somewhere on the same slab of granite that held the immutable rule about wanted items being on the bottom of available piles there surely was a closely related law proclaiming that any embarrassment that *could* happen surely *would* happen. Same author, same chisel.

So he figured the sensible thing would be to step out of sight before dropping his drawers.

In no great hurry he finished his smoke, then picked up his clothes and carried them down to the far end of the car where a stack of crates labeled MacEachern's Ready to Wear, Fine Fabrics at Reasonable Rates, extended nearly to the ceiling. A little pushing and shoving gave him room enough to slip in between the crates and the end wall of the boxcar.

Longarm dropped the stub of his cheroot onto the floor and ground it out underfoot, then took his things into the makeshift dressing room.

Uh huh. Damn good thing he'd slid out of sight, all right. He was still buttoning his shirt when he heard the door at the far end of the car open with a thump.

Longarm peered around the side of the crates and saw he needn't have been concerned. It was only the left-field player, Nat. Nathaniel something-or-other, actually.

Longarm quickly finished with the shirt and tucked it into his trousers, slipping his galluses over his shoulders and intending to step out and speak to the man.

Before he could do that, though, the door opened again

and a young man in regular clothes, not one of the ball players and no one Longarm had seen before, came into the car.

There was something about the two of them, Nat on the one hand and the newcomer on the other, that made Longarm freeze in place, watching them from his unintended hiding point nearby.

Although they obviously thought they were alone in the car Nat looked nervously about, as if to satisfy himself on that score.

Then Nat pulled his shirttail out of his baseball uniform trousers and reached beneath it for a packet he'd secreted inside his waistband.

The stranger responded by producing a small package of his own.

This was getting interesting-er and interesting-er, Longarm thought.

He wasn't a lick inclined to step out and show himself as just another of the boys now. He stayed where he was and watched as the two packets changed hands.

He had no idea what might be in the tiny box—or whatever—that Nat received. It could have been almost anything small enough to fit into a space roughly the size of a jewelry box.

But there wasn't a whole helluva lot of doubt in Longarm's mind about what Nat was giving to the other guy.

That flat little bundle was just exactly the size and shape of a tightly wrapped sheaf of currency. No telling how much was in there, of course. And no telling what for. But Longarm had no doubt in his mind, none, that Mr. Nathaniel whozitts was buying something here, or paying off a split, whatever, that he damn sure didn't want his teammates to know about.

And wasn't that downright interesting just minutes after Douglas McWhortle informed the team that they weren't gonna be paid for this ball game because some SOB went and stole all the gate receipts that they'd worked for these past days.

Real interesting indeed, Longarm thought.

He shifted to the back of the narrow niche behind the stack of crates and waited patiently for Nat and his pal to leave.

But he was thinking the whole while he waited.

Chapter 20

The next town on the schedule was a half-horse—it wasn't big enough to justify calling it one-horse—burg named Hoskin. It really seemed more a freight siding than a village, and as far as Longarm could tell there was neither local law to notify about potential danger nor anything for miles around worth stealing even if there had been a Hoskin police force.

The community consisted of a freight ramp and telegrapher's shack, but no actual station, and a grand total of two, count them, two, commercial establishments. One was a general mercantile, the other a smithy where plows and scythes and the like might be repaired, mules shod, and similarly exciting happenings take place.

Longarm doubted the community could muster enough people—never mind people with cash to spare—to bother staging a game before. But then the scheduling hadn't been his responsibility. Fortunately. A place like this, he figured, must surely be an embarrassment to Douglas McWhortle, who probably made up his touring schedule blind by mail or telegraph with no real idea what they would find when they got to some of these whistle-stop places.

When he mentioned something of the sort to the manager though, McWhortle only shrugged and said, "Let's wait and see what happens tomorrow afternoon."

At least there wouldn't be days of layover and practice in Hoskin, Longarm was pleased to note. For the next couple weeks the travel and the play would be almost nonstop.

"There isn't any hotel around here that I can see," he mentioned, politely, he thought.

"Don't worry, Short. We won't make you sleep on the ground."

"Alone, maybe, but not on the ground," the baby-faced young pitcher Dennis Pyle put in.

True to the manager's word, no one was obliged to sleep outdoors. As the ball players unloaded from the narrow gauge train there were folks gathering. Longarm suspected they were springing up from underground burrows or something because there damn sure didn't seem enough houses around to hold them all. But from whatever hidden sources they did appear. In twos and threes, by wagon and buggy and a good many afoot, the Hoskin folk gathered.

And one by one the Austin Capitals disappeared.

With no hotel or even a regular boardinghouse to accommodate them, the players were doled out among the townspeople and taken into private homes.

"We'll meet back here at noon tomorrow," McWhortle reminded each man before he was allowed to wander off with his host family. "The game is at one, lunch and team meeting before. Mind you don't be late."

Longarm received the same reminder as everyone else and was sent off on foot with a family that consisted of a huge, red-faced farmer named Hugo Schultz, his plump Frau Gertrude, and enough tow-headed kids in assorted sizes to make up their own ball team if they'd been so inclined . . . complete with substitutes and a smattering of pinch hitters if needed.

Hugo might not look like so much in his bib overalls and flannel union suit, Longarm thought, but the man was a potent breeder, that was for damn sure.

"Come now, Herr Short. Supper be on the table when we get home," Frau Schultz invited with a huge welcoming smile.

Longarm touched the brim of his Stetson and tried to

pick up his bag—it was snatched away from him by a young behemoth who at twelve or so looked like he could have carried the whole team's luggage, complete with rail station baggage cart, without raising a sweat—as he joined the family on their march home.

This could, he thought, prove to be much more comfortable than some sterile, impersonal hotel.

Chapter 21

"No thanks, I couldn't, really, it was mighty fine but I couldn't hold another bite, thank you." He damn near had to fight the girl off to keep her from adding another slab of pie to his plate. And good though the dried apple pie was, his belly was already groaning from the punishment it'd taken.

These Germans did know how to eat.

Frau Schultz had said the meal would be ready as soon as they got to the house, and the woman hadn't lied. The crowd that came into town to fetch home their own personal baseball player turned out to be only part of the Schultz clan. The rest of the bunch, the daughters, stayed at home cooking.

Actually, Longarm suspected, they and their mother, too, must've spent the last solid week doing nothing but preparing the meal they'd just stuffed into him.

It occurred to him, somewhat too late to do anything about it, that this whole thing might be a plot designed to incapacitate the visiting ball players. Make them all eat so much that they couldn't move and the amateur home club would have a walk-over come tomorrow afternoon. He decided he would check with the other boys in the morning to see if everyone of them'd been treated as rudely by their hosts as he had by the Schultz family.

In the meantime what he figured he needed was about a half hour rocking in one of those highback chairs he'd seen on the porch. A little rocking and a good smoke and maybe the pressure in his belly would ease up a mite. He stood, biting back a groan, with the thought in mind to excuse himself and make for the porch.

"It is late," Hugo announced before Longarm could speak. "Time now we close the doors unt vindows and all go to sleep, ja?"

If early to bed was the virtue it was cracked up to be, Longarm thought, then this bunch was virtue on the hoof.

But this wasn't his household to administer, and if old Hugo ordered everyone onto the sheets, then bedtime it would have to be.

Frau Schultz gave directions, obviously by prearrangement. Longarm was given the lean-to that normally housed the three daughters. The girls were sent up the ladder to the loft where the boys usually slept. And the boys were chased out to the hayloft where they no doubt would spend most of the rest of the night taking this opportunity to raise a little mild hell. Schultz *mère et père*—or whatever the German equivalent of that would be—had their own bedroom to disappear into and were the only ones on the farm who would be sleeping in their own beds this night.

Confusing, Longarm thought, but plenty gracious and considerate of them to treat a stranger so kindly. He thanked everyone in sight and retired to the lean-to.

He sank onto the rope-sprung bunk that looked the most sturdy of those available and took a look around by the light of the candle stub he'd been given. There wasn't much to see. The Schultz girls didn't have much in the way of fancies or doodads. A few woodcuts snipped out of magazines seemed to be the basis of their decor along with a few cornshuck dolls. The room, like the family, seemed modest enough.

What Longarm really wanted, but knew better than to hope for, was an ashtray. He settled for unlatching the shutter over the unglazed window—Hugo hadn't spent extra for foolishness like glass—with the intention of dropping

74

his ashes and cigar butt outside. Damned if he figured to go to sleep though without one more smoke.

It didn't take any time at all for the house to go silent once everyone settled down. Before Longarm was halfway through his cheroot he could hear loud snoring from the direction of the Schultzes' bedroom.

A few seconds later he heard the telltale creak of wooden ladder rungs as one of the girls came back down from the loft. Making a trip to the outhouse, Longarm figured. Then he realized he was mistaken as his bedroom door was drawn slowly open.

He could see the pale, ghostly shape of a nightdress as the girl stepped inside and quietly pushed the door closed behind her.

Longarm's eyes hadn't quite adjusted to the dark yet so it took him a few seconds to see that it was the oldest girl who'd come in uninvited and unannounced . . . unwanted, too, for that matter.

Her name was Trudy and she was the same one who'd been trying to fatten him like a hog for the slaughter all during supper.

Longarm guessed Trudy to be all of thirteen, maybe fourteen tops. She had dirty blond hair done up in plaits that were coiled and pinned to the sides of her head.

The girl had a long face and prominent teeth so that she reminded Longarm of a mule he'd once been forced to plow with when he was about the same age this girlchild was now. Come to think of it, when Trudy turned around and bent over the stove, her butt looked kind of reminiscent of that same mule.

Good mule. The pity was that Longarm didn't all that much care for mules.

Nor for thirteen-year-old kids no matter how infatuated and breathless they might be.

"Mr. Short."

75

"Evenin', Trudy. Forget something in your room that you need?" he suggested.

"No, I . . ."

"You're a good cook."

"Thank you." It was too dark for him to see her blush, but he could tell by the way she wrung her hands and turned her shoulders that she would be blushing hot as a coal-fired stove on a January night.

"You and your sisters and ma been mighty nice t' me. I'm grateful."

"I . . . Mr. Short . . . ?"

"Yes, Trudy?"

"I . . . I think you're the most fine and handsome gentleman I ever did see."

"Why, Trudy, that's real sweet of you t' say a thing like that. I appreciate it. I got t' tell you, child, that you're a mighty pretty girl too."

"Do you really think so?"

"I do, Trudy. I surely do."

"I think . . . I think . . . ." She let out a ragged, wrenching sob and galloped across the small room to throw herself into his arms and plant a wet, inexpert kiss square on his mouth. Longarm barely had time to snatch his cigar aside or she likely would've impaled her left nostril on the lighted end of it en route to his face. "I think you're just wonderful, Mr. Short." She kissed him again, with vigor if not with skill, and only winced a little bit when his whiskers sandpapered her skin.

"Mm, I sure didn't expect nothing like this, Trudy," he told her once he had the use of his lips back. Darn girl was breathing so heavy he thought she might be having some sort of climax all by herself there. That made him kinda jealous. But only a very little.

"I can't help myself, Mr. Short. You're just about the most handsome and wonderful man I ever did see."

"Why thank you, Trudy. An' you're a right fine figure

76

of a woman too. You, uh, are a woman already, aren't you?''

"I . . . what do you mean, Mr. Short?''

"I mean you're old enough to have your monthly time good an' regular, aren't you?''

She pulled back and gave him a quizzical look. "Not regular every month, no, but I've had my bleeding twice now already.'' She hesitated but couldn't stop herself from asking, "Why'd you want to know that, Mr. Short?''

"Excuse me for jumpin' the gun here, Trudy, but I kinda got the idea . . . I mean, what with you comin' in here t' my bedroom in the middle o' the night an' everything, all pretty an' sweet smellin' in that nightdress . . . I kinda got the idea that you was sweet on me.''

"Oh, I am, Mr. Short. I really am powerful sweet on you.''

"An' I feel the same, Trudy. Pretty as you are I just can't help myself. So naturally I have t' think, well, if we was to get together an' get married, we'd likely be havin' kids of our own on the way right away. If you're started havin' your monthlies, that is. You know how it is. Quick as a man an' woman start doin' that together the woman is sure to get her belly all swole up with kids, one poppin' out right after another. Next thing you know you'll have a clothesline full o' diapers an' a yard full of babies crawlin' in the dirt. But you won't have t' worry none. I make five dollars a week playing ball, some weeks ten dollars, an' I'll be home two weeks every three months or so. Long enough t' get you knocked up again so you won't be gettin' in no trouble while I'm away.'' He chuckled a bit and let some cigar smoke trickle out of his mouth so that it kind of accidentally wound up inside her nose.

Trudy coughed and pulled back a little way.

"Yep,'' Longarm said, "you sure are one fine-looking girl. Excuse me. Woman. You aren't no little girl any more. Or won't be after t'night, will you?'' He chucked her gently under the chin and dropped his hand to her lap where he began—rather clumsily—to grope her crotch.

Trudy recoiled, jumping off his lap and backing away toward the door. "Mr . . . Mr. Short, please."

"Did I say somethin' t' scare you, honey? Now I never meant t' do that. Come here, honey. Gimme a *big* kiss."

Trudy squealed. And bolted through the door, leaving it standing open as she scrambled up the ladder to the loft so fast he wasn't sure she bothered to use the rungs. She might just have flown up the thing.

Longarm laughed silently and took a few more puffs on his cigar. He finished it at his leisure and dropped the butt out the window, then eased the window shut again.

When he went to rise so he could close the door and go to sleep, he discovered that once more he was not alone.

This time his visitor was somewhat harder to see in that he was wearing a nightshirt made of some dark fabric.

"Evening, Hugo. I thought you was asleep."

"My wife, she is the sound sleeper. Not so, me."

"Uh huh." Longarm could still hear the buzzsaw drone of snoring coming from the Schultzes' bedroom.

"I got good ears, you know?"

"Uh huh."

"At first I don't know what you are doing. Then I do. Trudy, she feels good about herself now, ja?"

"I hope so. Nice kid. I didn't want to hurt her."

"Ja, so I understand. You want a little drink, Mr. Short? I got a bottle put by where the frau pretends she don't know where to find."

"I'd like that, Hugo. If you'd agree to call me, uh, Chester. I'd be proud t' have a drink with you. Uh, would you like a cigar t' go with our drink, Hugo?"

"That I vould, Chester. That I vould."

All in all, Longarm concluded afterward, his overnight stay with the Schultz family proved to be downright comfortable.

Chapter 22

Longarm couldn't believe it. There were half again as many people turned out to see the ball game here as there had been back in Medicine Lodge. And here there wasn't hardly town enough to justify stopping at.

"Why?" he asked, gesturing at the hundreds of people who stood, or sat on the grass, all around the flat pasture that was designated a playing field.

McWhortle grinned and looked around for a moment before answering. "It's something I caught onto a couple years ago. A crossroads like Hoskin here doesn't even get a circuit preacher but three, maybe four times a year. And there's no professional entertainment whatsoever. No traveling theater troupes or circuses, none of that. So when somebody does stop, somebody like us, *every*body comes out. We are the one and only big entertainment of the year, and there isn't a soul within ten or fifteen miles who would miss the chance to be here."

"I'll be damned," Longarm said in admiration and amazement. "It sure does work."

"Does for a fact, doesn't it? Assuming nobody steals the gate this time, that is."

"I'll kinda keep an eye on things if you like," Longarm offered.

"Do that," the manager hesitated half a second for emphasis, "Short. But you'll have to do it while you're busy with baseball too."

"What d'you mean?"

"I mean John Charles has a bellyache this morning. I understand the family he was with last night overfed him and he's miserable this morning. You'll play right field the whole game today." John Charles, J. C. Corcovan, was the regular right fielder. And in no danger whatsoever of being beaten out of his job by Custis Long.

"Sounds like a plot t' me," Longarm mumbled, remembering the tongue-in-cheek accusation he'd thought of about the Schultzes, fine folk that they were, last night.

"What?" McWhortle asked.

Longarm shook his head. "Nothing."

McWhortle grunted and walked off among the players, having a word with one here, giving a pat on the back there. He also pulled out his lineup and passed it around. Longarm discovered that he would be hitting ninth in the spot usually reserved for the pitcher . . . who was generally counted on to be the worst batter on the field. Longarm gathered that no one on the Capitals, including the manager, had a whole helluva lot of confidence in his abilities.

Which, he conceded, was probably downright sensible of them.

"Play ball," the Hoskin blacksmith and sometime baseball umpire shouted, and things got underway.

Longarm kept one eye on the tent where tickets and refreshments were being sold and the other eye on the Schultz crowd, the whole mob of which was sworn to cheer for their very own. Even a rather subdued Trudy timidly wished him luck early this morning, not knowing that her attempted first tryst had been overheard by her daddy the night before.

When Levi Watt grounded out to the Hoskin second baseman to end the top of the first inning, the Schultzes waved and shouted ferociously as Longarm trotted out onto the field. He felt like a warrior taking the lists on behalf of adoring patrons. Or something. For sure it made him want to do well so as to justify their faith in him.

And that made it all the more embarrassing when the third Hoskin batter hit a towering fly ball to right.

Longarm saw the little SOB come off the bat and sail his way. He knew it was coming. The problem was that he didn't have any idea just *where*.

He ran forward, decided that wasn't right and backpedaled, angled left a bit, then stopped and scuttled to his right. The damn ball just kept on coming.

It flew high, curled over in a picture-perfect arc, and plonked into the grass about fifteen feet to Longarm's left and a little way behind him.

By the time he caught up with it—fortunately it didn't roll far—the Hoskin runner was racing into third base. It was fortunate, too, that the runner didn't know what kind of arm he was facing out there in right field. Or he likely would have slowed to a walk and strolled on into home plate. As it was he hit the ground in a belly slide and tore up some grass as he reached the base with room to spare.

Longarm cussed and muttered some and pointedly avoided looking in toward where the Schultz kids were probably disappointed in their own personal hero now. Dammit.

Worse, the next Hoskin batter, much more by accident than by any sort of design, hit a weak little excuse-me that looped over the third baseman's head and dropped in yards short of Nat Lewis in left. The man Longarm let get on loped in to score the first run of the game and put Hoskin one up on the visitors. It was a run they wouldn't have gotten if J. C. had been in right field, and Longarm knew it.

The next inning went little better. The ball just wasn't flying where the Caps wanted, and the Hoskin yokels set them down one-two-three. Then to compound the insult, the Hoskin boys scored another run in the second when their batters pounded out an infield single followed immediately by a solid double to—where the hell else—right field. That one wasn't Longarm's fault. But he felt bad about it anyway.

In the third he came up to bat and, trying his double damnedest, struck out on three pitches.

"Those were balls you were swinging at, you know," McWhortle mentioned—casually to be sure—when Longarm got back to the bench.

"You wouldn't want me t' hit something an' spoil my reputation now, would you?" Longarm asked.

"Forgive me. I wasn't thinking."

"Well don't let it happen again."

Longarm did better his next time up. It took the Hoskin pitcher four tosses to strike him out. He considered that to be a definite sign of improvement.

By the time the eighth inning ended Longarm—fortunately the record books would reflect and posterity would record that all this was done by some jerk named Chester Short—had distinguished himself by striking out three times and dropping not one but two easy flies.

The Hoskin nine was leading the Austin Capitals by a score of six to four.

Longarm was commencing to hope the Schultzes had had to go home early to do chores so he wouldn't have to face looking into the eyes of those kids when the game was over.

In the top of the ninth Caleb Jones got on base with a walk and was moved over to second two batters later when Ted Carter reached on an error by the third baseman. Longarm was grateful to see that he wasn't the only one on the field capable of screwing up.

Dennis Pyle struck out, leaving the Caps with one remaining opportunity. And the next scheduled batter was that imbecile who called himself Short.

"You sending in a pinch hitter?" Longarm asked the bossman.

McWhortle shook his head. "Nope. We've all seen you

hit. Just relax and don't think about it. For some reason you've been tight all day. Trying too hard. Just relax and be yourself. You'll be fine.''

Longarm gave the manager a look that suggested maybe young McWhortle was losing his grip. But what the hell. He picked up a bat and went out there.

Some people in the crowd saw who the batter was and cheered like crazy. Longarm didn't think the voices were those of the Schultzes. Just some locals who had faith that with this guy at bat their victory was assured.

Longarm looked at the pitcher who was grinning at him from the mound. Well, why the hell wouldn't the guy be pleased? He'd struck Longarm out swinging three times in a row, hadn't he?

The first pitch came in low and so far outside Longarm probably couldn't have reached it with a broomstick, never mind a ball bat.

"Strike!" the blacksmith bellowed.

"You don't take no chances, do you," Longarm suggested in a low voice.

"Got something to say to me, mister?" the blacksmith shot back. "See me later if you're man enough."

Longarm turned and gave the fellow a cold look. The blacksmith was twice Longarm's size and solid muscle. Longarm grunted and turned back to face the pitcher. He hadn't come here to play that sort of game. It was bad enough he was required to play baseball in this summer heat. He sure as hell didn't need another brawl to shorten this contest.

"Strike!" the blacksmith roared after a pitch came so far inside it like to put a polish on Longarm's belt buckle.

Longarm looked back at the umpire and the guy gave him a snotty do-something-about-it look in return.

Whatever the next pitch turned out to be, Longarm figured, he would have to take a whack at it because it was sure as hell going to be a strike regardless.

83

The pitcher wound up and hurled the thing, and it came whistling in about belly high and square over the plate.

Longarm let his reflexes take over, just like McWhortle said he should.

The crack of horsehide on hardwood was crisp and sweet to hear, and the ball soared toward the clouds in search of eagles to fly with.

The Hoskin center fielder never bothered to take a step back. There were those who said later that the ball went so high and so far that it caused rain over a three county area and broke a critical drought. But Longarm wasn't sure if he should take credit for that or not.

The Caps won the game seven to six, and afterward Longarm found himself hip deep in small blond Schultzes clamoring to ride on the shoulders of their own personal hero.

Chapter 23

"Short."

"Yo, boss."

"I need you to run an errand for me."

"Sure thing, boss." Longarm let McWhortle draw him away from the rest of the boys, who were sitting on, over, around, and through a set of loading chutes waiting for a westbound train to carry them all to the next scheduled game.

"Trouble," the manager said in a low voice once they were away from the players.

"Not another theft of the gate receipts," Longarm said. "I mean, I wasn't watching every second, not hardly, but I never noticed. . . ."

"It wasn't that," McWhortle said, "but the Hoskin post office was broken into and robbed this afternoon."

"Shit," was Longarm's heartfelt opinion of the news.

"Yeah," McWhortle agreed. "Look, I thought you would want to go do, well, whatever it is you do in a situation like this."

"Hell, I didn't even know Hoskin was big enough to *have* a post office."

"It isn't much," the team boss explained, "just a counter and set of pigeonholes inside the mercantile. The proprietor, I suppose he's the postmaster, too, is the man who was in charge of the host committee. We went back to his store to count the gate and divvy up the money. That's when he found the break-in."

"I better go talk to him," Longarm said.

"While you're there you'd best pick up something that the boys can see you bring back to me since this is supposed to be an errand you're going on."

"Right."

"The train is due in an hour and a quarter."

"I'll be on time," Longarm promised.

The store was one of those crowded, dusty affairs that sells a little bit of damn near everything. There were plowshares and smoked hams hanging from the rafters, barrels of nails sitting beside barrels of flour, and bags of mortar piled next to bags of salt. There was corn oil, coal oil, whale oil, linseed oil, and oil of camphor. Bacon and bullet molds, hen eggs and darning eggs. Whatever a man needed he could likely find in Howard Jefson's store.

Except answers, that is.

"Who knew the store would be closed during the ball game?" Longarm asked.

"Everybody who does business here. Which includes everybody who lives within twenty miles of Hoskin," Jefson told him. "I've had a notice to that effect posted for at least the past month."

"So any local bad boy would have known the coast was clear," the marshal—he still felt like a clown in the baseball uniform, but there hadn't been time to change into something more befitting a United States deputy marshal in the pursuit of official duties—suggested.

"Sure," Jefson agreed, "but nobody has stolen anything around here since last fall. I mean nothing, marshal. Zero."

"This robbery last fall . . . ?" Longarm prompted.

Jefson grinned, and Longarm got the impression the local man had been waiting for just that question. "Lou and Agnes Brumbauer's five-year-old twins snitched some candy outa that jar over there. And that, mister, is the biggest crime we've had in Hoskin since the town was founded."

"If it comes t' that I suppose I can have the Brumbauer twins brought in for questioning," Longarm said with a deadpan expression, which earned him another grin and perhaps some approval from the storekeeper/postmaster/ball game organizer. "Seriously, d'you have any thoughts on who might've done this?"

"Seriously, I wish to hell that I did, marshal." Jefson shook his head and looked sadly around. "I lost a lot more than just the postal receipts, you know."

"I'm sure."

Whoever hit the post office broke in by the simple expedient of prying the back door open and walking in. The padlock that was supposed to secure the door was of top quality and in fact did the job it was designed to do. The lock remained strong and inviolate. Unfortunately the hasp it was supposed to secure snapped in two under the pressure of a prybar. The marks left by the bar—a big one—were clearly visible on the wooden doorframe.

"Easy as pie, wasn't it?" Longarm said.

"Too damned true, it was."

"They knew where the money was?" Longarm asked.

Jefson shrugged. "How could you tell? The store receipts were in a steel box under the counter there. That was obvious enough, and the whole box is gone. They didn't bother to try and break it open here, just picked it up and walked off with it. The post office money was in a cash drawer. You can see where they used the pry bar to snap that open. Again it wasn't exactly hard for anyone to spot, whether they'd been here before and knew the layout or if they were strangers coming in for the first time. The rest of it, more post office money, was in a bank bag that I'd hidden behind that ledger book on the shelf there." He pointed. "But I suppose a cursory look would turn that up, too. I mean, I just hadn't thought in terms of securing things from robbers. Not until the Brumbauer kids get tall enough to see over the counters, anyhow."

"Yeah, I see what you mean. How about your local law? Where's your town marshal?"

"Don't have one. Why, we don't even have a deputy assigned to this part of the county. There's the county sheriff, of course, but the only reason he ever needs to come around is when he's electioneering, giving speeches and asking for votes. Fourth of July there's usually one of the county supervisors will show up and give a talk, but except for that we don't have much dealing with government."

"Have you sent for a deputy?"

"Sure. Likely one of the boys will come over tomorrow sometime. Or the next day."

Longarm sighed. There wasn't a hell of a lot to see here.

He went outside, starting at the front and working his way around the building. The alley at the back where the door was broken open was littered with trash on ground that was hard as macadam. A herd of circus elephants wouldn't have left tracks on soil that thoroughly compacted, and if there were any footprints to be seen then they would have to be spotted by someone an awful lot better than Custis Long. And in truth he didn't think there *was* anyone that much better than he.

"Do you know if anyone saw anything or anyone, well, out of the ordinary? Today? Any time in the past week? Anything at all?"

Jefson shook his head. "Not that I know of."

"Then I expect we'll have to ask around," Longarm said. He thought about the train that was soon due in to carry the Capitals on to their next stop. He was supposed to be on that train.

On the other hand, his job here, appearances aside, was to act as a U.S. deputy marshal and never mind the silliness of baseball.

If he had to, he figured, he could ask the Schultzes to put up with him for one more night.

"Let's go look for folks t' talk to," he told Jefson.

88

Chapter 24

No way in hell was Longarm going to get on that train, by himself, in broad daylight, wearing a baseball uniform. He said his latest round of good-byes to the Schultz clan and got Howard Jefson to open his store shortly past dawn the next morning so Longarm could shuck the uniform and dress himself in a fifty-cent cotton shirt, a dollar pair of used Levis, and a two-bit soft cap. The price seemed a mite stiff. But preferable to spending the day being stared at by total strangers.

The train ride, thanks to his badge, didn't cost anything though, and that was something.

He settled onto the cinder-pocked cushions of a seat in the smoking car and enjoyed a cheroot while he pondered the little he'd learned from his unexpected overnight extension in Hoskin.

It hardly seemed worth the bother.

Jefson had had time to go over his records and as far as the man could determine he'd lost a little over eight hundred in store receipts plus something in excess of twelve hundred in postal funds. The total take in the break-in was close to twenty-one hundred.

As for who might have done it, they hadn't learned much of anything.

No one Longarm and Jefson talked to the previous evening remembered seeing anything or anyone out of the ordinary of late.

The only strangers reported were a threesome of cowboys seen camping in a live oak grove along a stream the locals called Three Mile Creek. And Milt Warner, the farmer who saw them, said they seemed innocent and ordinary as could be.

"Did they try and hide from you when you spotted them?" Longarm had asked Warner.

"Naw, not a bit of it. In fact when I first seen them they was waving to me. They was cooking some squirrels they'd shot, making a right nice-smelling stew, and first thing they done was invite me to eat with them. They mistook the land for mine and asked permission to spend the night there. I told them to go ahead and bed down, that I knew Ralph . . . he's the fellow owns that piece of ground . . . I told them I knew Ralph wouldn't mind and for them to make themselves to home. They said they was on their way home in Texas someplace . . . I forget exactly where they said they was from . . . after delivering a herd of stock cows to a fellow up near Manhattan."

"I thought the days of cattle drives being welcome in Kansas were over," Longarm said.

"Beef shipping is pretty much done with because of the fevers those Texas cows bring with them. But if a man don't mind the time and money to have his cattle dipped for ticks and inspected he can still make out selling breeding stock. The steers they mostly drive on the government trails on west of here, but there's a good market yet for breeders," Warner explained. "I bought some myself off a fella from Beeville, Texas, just, let me see, two years back it will be this August. Decent cows too. They accept my bulls just fine and have easy birthing with them fine-boned little calves. Little buggers grow fast once they're on the ground, too. Convert their feed real nice, they do."

The farmer was obviously more interested in talking about livestock and probably crops, too, than he was in the things that were of interest to Longarm.

As for the cowboys, he'd shrugged and said they seemed

like nice young fellows to him and he hadn't any reason to be suspicious of them, not then and not now.

"They was carefree young'uns, not a mean bone among the three of them is what I'd say," Warner concluded. "I wouldn't think of them in connection with anything like Jefson's robbery."

Longarm pretty much had to agree. After all, the cowboys had been in the vicinity of Hoskin two days ago. At pretty much the exact same time the ticket receipts were being stolen down in Medicine Lodge.

And considering the string of previous thefts, he had to figure all of the incidents were connected.

He slumped in a corner of the swaying smoker bench and sucked on his cheroot.

The only real suspect he had—and that was on thin ground—was Nat Lewis and his mysterious meetings on two separate occasions.

But, dammit, Longarm himself saw Nat involved tooth and toenail in the brawl with the locals down in Medicine Lodge. And the man was right there on the ball field in plain view of Longarm and about five hundred other citizens at the approximate time the Hoskin post office was being broken into.

A man would have to work real hard at knitting those facts into a blanket of guilt.

Longarm scowled at the ash on his cigar and conceded that the only thing he knew for certain sure was that he didn't know hardly anything.

He closed his eyes and waited for the Plains and Pacific to catch him up with the rest of the team.

Chapter 25

"Where in hell have you been, you miserable, skirt chasing, ball dropping son of a lowlife bitch?" The team manager winked at Longarm—which the rest of the boys weren't in a position to see—and expanded considerable on the theme already established.

Chet Short, it seemed, was due for a proper tongue-lashing for missing yesterday's train out of Hoskin.

After several minutes of loud invective—pretty good stuff, too, if Longarm did say so—McWhortle appeared to calm down a mite. He snatched Longarm by the elbow and led him off a little ways, dropping his voice so the others could no longer hear although they continued to look on in amusement and no doubt also in some appreciation for the fact that it was this Denver newcomer who was getting the needle and not themselves.

Once they were well clear of the team members, Mc-Whortle said in a perfectly calm and controlled tone, "Sorry, but I think you understand."

Longarm nodded and tried to maintain the look of a man who was in the process of getting his ass chewed.

"How did it go yesterday?"

"Didn't learn much, dammit. No clues t' who's behind all this."

"None at all?"

Longarm shook his head without having to give the question so much as a moment's thought. And if he happened to have a suspicion or two, well, that wasn't anything like being the same as having an actual suspect. And if he did come up with a genuine suspect it still wouldn't be any of Douglas McWhortle's nevermind.

The truth was that Longarm thought McWhortle was straight and clean.

But he didn't exactly know that for a certain fact, did he.

And about the only human being U.S. Deputy Marshal Custis Long would be willing to confide unconfirmed suspicions with would be United States Marshal William Vail, anyhow.

Longarm wasn't even tempted to mention the strange goings-on involving Nat Lewis.

Not until or unless they turned out to mean something.

"What's the deal with this place here?" he asked instead of responding to the manager's question.

"The game is tomorrow afternoon at half past noon. This time in a field behind the livery stable over there." McWhortle pointed. "You already missed lunch, I'm afraid, and the boys would find it very strange if I offered to buy you a meal off the menu. We won't eat again until eight tonight. In the hotel dining room, of course. They will have a big table set up for us."

"Can't get in any earlier'n that?" Longarm asked. He hadn't eaten on the train and could feel the beginning of some rumbling in his gut.

"Go in and order something any time you're willing to pay for it yourself," McWhortle said. "But the price I worked out for the ball club says we all eat together and all get the same dinner."

"Cheap," Longarm said.

"Cheap," McWhortle concurred.

Longarm knew what that would mean. A hotel equivalent of boardinghouse food. Lots of starches and damn little in the way of meats or sweets. Beans, potatoes, gravy made sticky with too much flour. Yeah, a prospect like that would

93

make a man's mouth water all right. "We gotta practice this afternoon?" he asked.

"Of course. We were just getting ready to go over to the field. Jerry left with the equipment already."

"Any way I could get out of it?"

McWhortle frowned. Legitimately this time, Longarm thought. "Too tired from last night's acrobatics with some amateur whore?"

Longarm gave the young baseball manager a steely look to put the fellow in his place. "I got work t' do, y'know, that don't involve grown men playing at kids' games."

"I don't want the boys to think you're being rewarded after you missed the train yesterday."

"Then whyn't you get so pissed off that you suspend me for a game or two? You know. Get all red in the face an' scream some more an' jump up an' down where they can see. I'll get pissed off right back at you an' storm off an' not come back until suppertime tonight or about then. Would that work so's you wouldn't lose any control over your team?"

"That would be all right," McWhortle decided after a moment's thought. He hesitated a few seconds more, then winked at Longarm and took a deep breath.

When the man cut loose it was a marvel to behold.

He raved. He shouted. He got so red in the face that Longarm became concerned for his health. If Longarm hadn't known for certain sure that the whole thing was a sham, he might've felt impelled to beat hell out of the man in return for all the abuse McWhortle was dishing out.

But there was no question the two of them once again had the full attention of the Austin Capitals ball players.

Oh, it was a fine show McWhortle put on, Longarm thought.

And after a couple, three minutes of it Longarm commenced to shouting back and getting hot in the cheeks himself and pretty soon the two of them had worked themselves into a truly fine faretheewell.

They jumped and ranted and waved their arms about and when Longarm thought it had all gone on long enough and then some he shrieked a few well chosen insults, made as if barely restraining himself from punching out the manager, and with a flourish turned and stomped off down the street.

The last thing he saw as he turned away was Douglas McWhortle's wink and, he thought, a flicker of silent laughter in the young fellow's eyes.

Chapter 26

"Fifty cents," the man behind the counter said.

"Shouldn't that be . . . ?"

"Nickel apiece or fifty cents for the dozen. But thanks for being honest."

Longarm very happily fished two quarters out of the change in his pocket, hesitated only half a second or so and laid down a silver dollar instead. "At that price, friend, I'll take another dozen."

"I see you're a man who knows quality when he sees it." The clerk, and presumably proprietor as well, counted out another dozen of the slim cigars, bundled the purchase together and wrapped them in brown paper that he tied with string, careful not to damage the delicate tubes within.

The cheroots had such a pale and pretty leaf that it probably should be illegal, or at the very least immoral, to set fire to one. Which Longarm suggested to the storekeeper.

"Prob'ly would be a jailable offense except they taste even better than they look," the fellow said. "Here, try one."

"I don't. . . ."

"Go ahead, mister, this one's on the house." The man insisted, so Longarm let his arm be twisted. The storekeeper joined him in sampling the wares, and Longarm held a match so each of them could light up.

"By damn, it does taste even better than it looks."

"Have I ever lied to you, friend?" asked the man Longarm never saw in his life before this moment.

"Never once," Longarm answered solemnly.

The storekeeper drew deep on his smoke and smiled, and Longarm couldn't much help doing the same when he inhaled the smooth, flavorful smoke.

"Thinkin' of jailable offenses," Longarm ventured.

"Uh huh?"

"Do you have a jail hereabouts? Town marshal? Police department? Whatever?"

"Yes, we do, and I thank you for asking." The storekeeper took another puff on his cheroot.

"Would you please tell me where I can find such a place or person then?"

"That I would, mister. You go . . ." Longarm began paying less attention to the cigar and more to the instructions.

"Boone Crockett," the man with the badge on his shirt said by way of introduction as he leaned across the desk with a hand extended.

Longarm couldn't help but blink. But he didn't say anything. That would have been rude.

"It's all right, I know what you're thinking, and I expect you're right. It's a damned strange name at that. My daddy, he had this fascination with the old-time longhunters. You know the term?"

"I do," Longarm conceded.

"If you know the word then you know who those men were. My daddy, he claimed our line was descended from them. He never found any proof of it, but that didn't stop him from believing it was so. Didn't stop him from burdening me with this name either." The town marshal—Longarm was close enough now to read the lettering engraved onto the six-pointed star—shrugged and sat back down. "Now that we have that outa the way," he said, "what can I do for you?"

Longarm completed the other half of the introductions and said, "I have reason to think there is a good possibility some cash-heavy business in your town will be robbed to-morrow afternoon between twelve thirty and, oh, three o'clock or thereabouts.''

"If you wanted my interest, friend, you sure as hell got it." Crockett leaned forward, elbows on the desktop now and his attention rapt.

"Good because I'm hoping that between us we can do something about it. Stop any robbery from taking place here and nail whoever has been committing a string of others over the past couple months."

"Deputy, I can promise you one thing. Whatever help you think you need, me and my deputies will be glad to oblige you in supplying it."

"I appreciate your attitude, marshal. Look, uh, would you like a cigar?"

Boone Crockett smiled and accepted the cheroot Longarm held out to him. And just to be sociable, Longarm helped himself to another also even though he'd just gotten finished with one.

"Now," Longarm said. "Let's you and me do some serious talking. . . ."

Chapter 27

"Well, one thing's for sure," Crockett said. "Tonight we got to go to the cathouse."

"Pardon me?"

"Cathouse. Means whorehouse. Same thing."

"Hell, Boone, I know that, but . . ."

"Now I don't know how it is where you come from, Longarm, but around here we don't have much in the way of amusements for strangers to enjoy. Two saloons and one cathouse, that's all we got."

"I still don't see . . ."

"Been my experience, Longarm, that in a small town like this one here, anything a lawman wants to know about strangers passing through, he'll find it best in one of those two saloons or, more likely, in Belinda Joy Love's cathouse."

"Belinda Joy Love?"

"Oh, it ain't her real name, of course. I happen to know that that's Hilary Jean Thurmond. That's the way she's listed on the county tax rolls. I mean, everybody thinks she's just hired on by some man to run the cathouse for him, but the fact is she owns the property outright. She even talks about this made-up boss whenever she wants to duck the blame for some unpopular policy or whatever. But I know different." Crockett closed his eyes while he took another drag on the cigar Longarm had given him, then said, "We ought to drop by there about ten thirty–eleven o'clock."

"And you think she will cooperate?" Longarm asked.

Crockett opened his eyes and smiled. "I can pretty much guarantee it, my friend. Belinda Joy Love and me got what you might call an understanding."

"Whorehouses, cathouses that is, being in violation of the law hereabouts," Longarm suggested. It wasn't all that wild a guess.

"There's a county ordinance to that effect, yes," Crockett said cheerfully. "But no town statute, you see."

"An interesting distinction."

"Useful." Crockett looked close to swooning with the pleasure of his cigar. He blew smoke rings into the air, a dozen or more of them that hung over his head like so many errant halos drifting on the still air inside the marshal's office.

"You'll recall that I don't want anyone to know that I work for Marshal Vail," Longarm said. "Far as the civilians, or even your officers, are concerned I'd prefer to be thought of as just another one of the ball players from Texas."

"I thought of that, but you and me aren't so far apart in age. And I've spent some time in Texas, too, which folks here know about but have mostly forgiven me for. I intend to introduce you as an old friend from Bexar, which is where I used to work back before I learned that a man can sometimes make more by sitting on his ass than he can by letting a string of bad horses pound it or a herd of mossyhorn cows try and puncture it." He grinned. "You know something, Longarm? I haven't thrown a rope nor wrestled a calf since the day I figured that out. Ever been to Bexar?"

Longarm nodded. "Enough to tell a convincing lie if anybody questions me on it."

"That's who you are then. What's the name you said you're using with those overgrown children in tight pants?"

"Chester Short. But my friends call me Chet."

100

"Right. Chet it is, old pard. You and me rode together for Dad Waters at the Rafter D."

"I remember it well," Longarm said.

"Good. That settles that." Crockett pulled an onion-shaped watch from his pocket and consulted it. "We got a mite of time to kill," he said. "Tell you what. We'll have supper at my place. My old woman always cooks enough that there's extra in case company comes by. Then later on we'll stop in the saloons and have a beer or something at each one. To see if there's any new faces there. If there are I'll put one of my boys to keeping an eye on them. Once it's late enough then we'll go have that little talk with Belinda Joy Love and find out for certain if there's a bunch of strangers in town and if they are, what they're up to."

"Or what they claim to be up to anyhow," Longarm said.

"Which sometimes is good enough," Crockett said. "Sometimes you can learn about as much from a man's lies as you can from his truths, just so you know when it is that he's lying to you. You know what I mean?"

Longarm nodded.

"You hungry, friend Chet?"

"I feel about as empty as a bee tree with the hive smoked out of it."

Crockett stood and reached for his hat. "Let's go see what my old lady has on the stove, Chet."

Chapter 28

Boone Crockett's old woman was enough to melt a man into a puddle of steaming sweat. Or at least she made Custis Long feel like that.

He guessed her age at seventeen or thereabouts, a Mexican girl with a somewhat selectively slim body. Slim, that is, in selected portions. And anything but small in others. She had a chest that would have served admirably for any smith's furnace bellows and a round and pretty butt that looked stony cold perfect for the birthing of babies.

She had a pert and lovely face, cheekbones high enough to suggest more than a smattering of Indio hiding high in the branches of the family tree and lips that looked so hot it was a wonder there weren't brand marks all over Crockett. Or hell, maybe there were. But in places he didn't show around for just everybody to see.

Her hair was sleek and glossy and fell to someplace south of her waist. Which Longarm suspected could be spanned by a pair of warm hands.

Not that he would ever find out.

"Miz Crockett." He bowed and swept his Stetson off, which drew a dimpled smile from the town marshal's old lady. "Mister Short," she said in response as Crockett was going along with the fiction of Longarm's identity even at home now. "Welcome."

Longarm glanced sideways toward his new friend and saw something of a sparkle in the man's eyes. Ol' Crockett knew what he had here and was damned proud of it. Well, no wonder. Longarm reckoned he would have been, too, if he'd gotten himself a new playtoy as fine as this one.

"I hope you'll settle for potluck," Crockett said.

"Whatever you have," Longarm answered, knowing that Crockett's pleasures at home need have nothing to do with food.

"Juana, put a plate on for Mr. Short if you please."

"It is already done, *cara*. Mama saw you coming up the street with your guest. She had the place fixed before you reached the door. Go wash now. You too, Mr. Short. Hurry or everything will be cold and ruined before it reaches your plate, no?"

When they went into the kitchen, Longarm saw what Crockett meant earlier when he said there wouldn't be any danger of them running out of food even if a guest hadn't been announced ahead of time.

There were pots, platters, and steaming plates enough to feed half the town and still have scraps left over to throw to stray dogs.

And there were more than enough folks on hand to get around it all. He got lost midway through the introductions but in addition to Boone and Juana Crockett there were Juana's father and mother and sister—not but ten or eleven now but with a dark-eyed beauty whose appeal might someday rival her sister's—and three younger brothers and four or so cousins and . . . hell, Longarm gave up trying to figure out who they all were. He put the total number somewhere above twenty, the total only a rough estimate due to the ambled comings and goings through a busy back door, and left it at that.

No wonder Crockett hadn't been concerned about adding a mouth at the table.

Besides, he probably liked having someone around who spoke English. Crockett claimed to have no Spanish, and most of Juana's people either had no English or hid the knowledge right well if they did understand it.

103

Crockett and his guest were given places at the kitchen table along with Juana and her parents. Everyone else seemed to wander in, fill a plate and saunter back out again. It was purely amazing the quantities of food that disappeared over the course of the meal.

"That was good," Crockett said at length, reaching out to give his wife a pat on the backside as she carried a bowl of refritos to the table. People were still coming and going, and Longarm wasn't sure but that some of the faces belonged to fresh visitors. Juana beamed and paused long enough to wiggle her pretty butt at him before completing her task. Shy she was not. Happy though. Longarm guessed that Crockett and his child bride got along uncommonly well despite the presence of the army of relatives that came along with the package.

After supper, seated in rocking chairs on the front porch with a pair of Longarm's excellent stogies providing some stomach-soothing smoke, Crockett leaned back and explained, "Best damn thing that ever happened to me, finding Juana."

"So it looks like," Longarm agreed.

"I never had much family. My ma died early, giving birth to what would've been a brother. After that there was just me and my daddy and the stories he'd read to me about all the old-time heroes. I'm not complaining, mind. My daddy was a good man and he did his best for me. But I like having a big family. And they like knowing I want to take care of them all. Anyway, we get along pretty good, all of us."

"Nice folks," Longarm said diplomatically, "and your wife is lovely."

"She is, isn't she. Been married almost a year now." He winked. "Time we start thinking about having a kid of our own to add to the stew."

Longarm wasn't quite sure how to respond to that so he settled for pulling some smoke out of his cheroot. Damn,

104

but this was an uncommon fine batch of cigars he'd blundered into.

"Juana!" Crockett raised his voice only a little, but within seconds the girl was at the door to see what her husband needed. "Yes, dear?"

"Me and Chet will be going over to the cathouse soon as we're done smoking. You wanta ask that brother of yours if he'd like to get laid tonight?"

Juana giggled and disappeared.

Longarm wasn't entirely sure if the question was a tease . . . or if it might actually be serious.

Crockett grinned. "Relax, Short. Juana knows how I work. Besides, it was Belinda Joy Love that sold her to me in the first place."

The man waited for Longarm's confusion to run full course across his features—Crockett was not disappointed in what all he might see there, Longarm was sure—then said, "Juana and her folks were part of a traveling harvest crew. Her little sister got sick and needed doctoring, which the SOB in charge of the outfit ran into a big debt. Which he discharged by selling Juana to Belinda Joy Love. Belinda Joy, bless her moss-covered heart, isn't half bad. She knew Juana didn't deserve any such, so she called me in on the deal. Amongst us we prosecuted that son of a bitch. He's in the pen now making little ones outa big ones and likely cussing me, Juana, and Belinda Joy Love every morning he wakes up. Me, I took one look at Juana and fell hard. Would've married her right on the spot that first day I ever seen her. As it happened, though, she made me wait six whole weeks while her mama got her dress sewed and her father got sober after all the celebrating. We been a family ever since."

"And the brother?"

"Oh, that was Carlos I was talking about. Carlos is fifteen. Horny little bugger like all kids are at that age. He thinks he's in love with one of the girls at Belinda Joy

Love's place, and he'd do anything to spend a little time there. Which his pa thinks is about the funniest thing he's ever heard of. The whole family teases the poor kid, though sometimes I think it'd be better to take him over there and let him try it on for size one time.''

Longarm finished his cheroot and flipped the butt out into the yard.

"Let's go do some work, old pard. You remember who you are?"

"Hell, yes," Longarm said. "You and me rode together down Bexar way. For a fella name of Dad Waters on the Rafter D."

"*Bueno*. Let's go catch us some bad guys, eh?" Crockett took a final deep puff on his cigar and tossed it away into the gathering dusk. "Just follow me, old friend, and agree with whatever I say." He winked. "Especially if I need you to pay my gambling debts."

Longarm laughed and followed Crockett off the porch and back in the direction of the town center.

Chapter 29

"Dammit, Boone, you ain't gonna take him away from the table now, are you? Your friend's the big winner. It ain't right for you to take away our chance to get even."

Crockett shrugged but didn't change his mind, and Longarm began scooping up the loose change piled in front of him. He and four other townsmen, all friends of the local law to one degree or another, had been marking time by playing penny-ante poker. And Longarm hoped the protest from the player to his left wasn't serious or the poor fellow had no business sitting in at even a low stakes contest like this one. Longarm's "big" winnings didn't amount to much more than a dollar, he was sure, and that was after an hour and a half of desultory play.

Apparently, though, it was late enough now that Longarm and Crockett could go on over to the whorehouse for that little talk with Crockett's source of information there.

Longarm hoped that visit was more productive than the town saloons had turned out to be. The only drinkers and card players to be found this evening were local or near-local men, farmers, and a very few stockmen, who either lived in town or close enough to ride in for the baseball game that would be played tomorrow.

No strangers had shown themselves so far, suspicious or otherwise.

"After you, Chet," Crockett said, gesturing toward the door.

Longarm nodded to the fellows he'd been playing against

and ambled out, a cheroot clamped in his jaw.

"Still no word about anyone you don't know?" Long-arm asked.

"Not a soul. But if there is anyone new in town, Belinda Joy will know about it," Crockett promised.

The town marshal led the way to a low, sprawling building that looked more like a warehouse than a whorehouse. Despite the late hour, however, a lamp burned at the entry, and there were half a dozen horses and driving rigs waiting in the shadows. Considering the likely number of walk-up customers, it seemed Miss Love did a thriving trade.

"Popular," Longarm observed.

"The only place in the whole county where a man can be sure of getting his ashes hauled instead of having his face slapped," Crockett said.

"Licensed?"

"Hell, no. County commission wouldn't stand for any such a notion. They'd be thrown out of office before the ink was dry on any ordinance that would approve this debauchery and degradation. And the town council stays out of it altogether. They don't want the aggravation."

"I see," Longarm said, suspecting that indeed he did.

"Illegal as anything can be. Belinda Joy is arrested . . . so to speak . . . and pays fines on Monday mornings, regular as clockwork. Twenty dollars for the house and four dollars for each girl." Crockett smiled. "Belinda Joy is very civic-minded. She keeps our taxes down to an affordable level, and the decent ladies have the satisfaction of knowing that their morals are protected by force of law."

"Everyone is happy," Longarm said.

"Let's hope so." Crockett tapped lightly on the door to Belinda Joy Love's house of happiness.

Belinda Joy Love would have needed high heels, and maybe have to go up on her tiptoes as well, to make it to five feet of altitude. She was a tiny wee china doll of a woman. With perhaps a few age cracks in the porcelain. Heavy makeup was not enough to cover the wrinkles that the years had bred around her mouth and eyes nor diminish the wattles that formed beneath her chin.

Even so one could see what a fine figure of a little woman she must have been twenty, thirty years ago.

Her natural hair color by now must surely be white, but that fact was rather artlessly concealed with hennaed red. Her eyes were bright blue, though, and that was certainly natural enough. She smiled when she saw Boone Crockett and welcomed him and his friend Chet inside.

"So nice to see you, dear." She pulled Crockett's face down to see-level so she could give him a buss on the cheek, then extended a soft hand and a seemingly genuine greeting to Longarm as well. "It is a pleasure to meet you, dearie. You know the old saying, Any friend of Boone's is . . . you know the rest, of course."

"Yes, ma'am." The "ma'am" part of that came out unexpected. He just couldn't help himself. There was something about this aging bawd that Longarm found he just plain liked. She smiled, exposing a set of choppers so white and perfect they had to be false, and reached up to pat Longarm lightly on the cheek. He couldn't believe she did that. It made him feel about twelve years old. "My pleasure, ma'am." And he meant it.

"Chester Short, is it? Is that what you said, Boone dear?"

"That's right, Belinda Joy. Chet and I rode together down in Texas a few years back. You remember. I've told you all about that."

"Of course, dear. So you did." Belinda Joy turned to a girl—not a bad-looking girl at that, thirty or thereabouts with outsized tits hanging from a skinny frame—and said, "Joycelyn, darling, be a sweetie and bring a pot of tea to my office. Also a bottle of our best rye whiskey and some of those small cigars we got from Sammy." She smiled

109

sweetly. "And mind you don't forget the lemon and sugar, dear."

"Yes, ma'am, right away." Joycelyn scurried off toward the back of the house while Belinda Joy motioned her guests away to the right, through a parlor that was furnished rather sumptuously for such an unimposing exterior, and on down a short corridor to a walnut-paneled office that held a large desk, a settee, and four quite elegant wingback chairs.

"Sit there please, Boone. And you over there please, marshal."

"Ma'am?"

Belinda Joy clapped her hands in joy and said, "Really, boys. Shame on both of you. Chester Short? I'd be a poor sort of crotchety old lawbreaker if I couldn't recognize the famous U.S. Deputy Custis Long, wouldn't I? Please don't worry, though. I won't give your game away, dear, whatever it may be. And please forgive me my conceit. I didn't want either one of you to think this old woman can be so easily taken in although I really should have remained silent, I suppose. I. . . ." She was interrupted by a tapping at the heavy oak door. She raised her voice. "Yes?"

Joycelyn came in carrying one tray, followed by a really stunning Mexican girl with another.

"Thank you, ladies." Belinda Joy oversaw the distribution of goodies—cigars to both gentlemen, tea to herself and Crockett, and a truly excellent distillation of rye whiskey for Longarm; the old bat really did seem to know what she was about—then prudently waited for the whores to depart before she toasted her guests and, still smiling, asked, "Now, boys. How may I help you?"

Chapter 30

Longarm stifled an almost overwhelming urge, quite naturally made all the more insistent because he didn't dare give in to it, to sneeze. It was dusty as hell in the attic, the tiny motes swirling and twisting in the heavy, still air.

And hot? Lordy, he did reckon. Sweat soaked every stitch he was wearing and plastered the cloth tight to his overheated flesh all sticky and itchy. He removed his Stetson and laid it aside. Which was something of a relief from the heat that held his head in a furnace but which also made it possible for the sweat on his forehead to stream through his eyebrows to collect in his eye sockets where it stung and burned. He used an already sodden handkerchief to mop and swab at the offending perspiration but what he needed wasn't a lousy hanky; what he needed was a tub—cold water, not hot—and a Turkish towel thick enough to require two to handle it. All right, a big towel and maybe a small Turkish girl to go with it. That should be all right.

Accepting the inevitable with a sigh, Longarm laid his cheek momentarily against the buttstock of the beat-up old borrowed shotgun he was cuddling—he'd left his own fine Winchester in Denver since baseball players wouldn't logically go a-traveling with so much armament to hand—and fought against an urge to close his eyes. In addition to everything else the heat in the damned attic was making him sleepy.

A little discomfort, though, would mean nothing if it allowed them, Longarm and the local boys, to catch the gang of thieves that seemed to be trailing alongside the Austin Capitals.

Last night Belinda Joy Love filled them in on the probabilities. There were indeed strangers in the neighborhood. Two of them. Young. Call it nineteen or twenty. One with yellow hair and the other with close-cropped brown hair. Lean, both of them, and not too tall. Horny as only the young can be horny and eager to release all that energy. Or so Belinda Joy's girls reported. The girls would have related the exact preferences of the newcomers also except neither Longarm nor Boone Crockett gave a damn.

The information that Long and Crockett did value was the fact that each of the young men, one called Jim and the other Joey, each claimed that he was on the verge of coming into sudden money. And claimed as soon as they made their hits—their own words according to the whores—as soon as they did that they would be back with cash enough to buy the girls out for a whole night long and then they would have some *real* fun.

Forewarned with those tidbits of braggadocio, Longarm, Crockett, and Crockett's two deputies were now intent on making sure there was no big hit to enrich the pockets of those two strangers in town.

There was no bank in town, not as such, but the largest mercantile offered storage boxes inside a massive steel safe. Boone Crockett had chosen to guard that one himself, hiding inside a closet where he could watch the seemingly unprotected safe without being observed.

The town marshal placed one of his deputies inside each of the saloons as well on the theory that those cash-heavy businesses would make for tempting targets if robbers wanted an easy score while the businesses were closed and all the townspeople out on the edge of town watching the ball game.

And Longarm, not in uniform for the day thanks to his "suspension" by a supposedly angry club manager, took

112

upon himself the task of protecting the United States Post Office.

Which was why he found himself lying in a hot and dusty and quite thoroughly miserable attic while his substance oozed out of his pores and trickled clean away.

Never, never, ever! had he been so hot or so uncomfortable. Not ever his whole life long.

He stifled an impulse to sneeze and another to scratch and wished those miserable little sonuvabitch robbers would walk in so he would have the satisfaction of making some-damn-body *pay* for this.

Chapter 31

Ha! Gotcha, you little SOB, Longarm thought as he heard a scratching at the side door, the faint creak of unoiled hinges, and soon the sound of slow, tentative bootsteps on the plank flooring.

Longarm strained to see what was going on down below. He was lying next to the ornate metal grillwork that covered the hole where, in other more comfortable times of the year, a stovepipe could be installed.

As it was he could see down into the post office but only at a sharp angle that covered a very limited field of vision. Still, he had a perfectly fine, almost directly overhead view of the post office safe. And that was what it was all about.

He heard the soft scrape of boot soles on wood, then a small clattering sound that he could not identify. No matter.

He debated whether to use the shotgun or his revolver once the robbers appeared beneath him. The shotgun would be awkward to bring into play in these close quarters but lethal when used. The Colt was more selective. Either way he would have to snatch the grate off in order to shoot down at anyone trying to break open the safe. And since one hand would be needed to pull the grate aside, perhaps he would be better off using the revolver. Careful to do it in silence, he laid the shotgun gently down and slid the big double action Colt out of his holster.

Now all he needed was for the robbers . . .

"Marshal?"

Longarm blinked. Who the hell?

"Mr. Short?" the same voice called again, a little louder this time. "Where are you, sir?" The was a sound like a cupboard being opened and closed again. "Marshal Crockett said for me t' come tell you there's nothing doing, sir. Ball game's over and everybody is on their way back. Those two boys you was warned about was out at the ball field along with everybody else, Boone says. Miz Joy sent a girl to tell him. They was out there drinking beer and eating peanuts and yelling like hell for that Texas team t' win, sir. Uh, wherever you are."

The local deputy was wandering around inside the post office while he spoke, directing his words to the counters and cabinets and into a broom closet so small it would barely hold a mop. Obviously the boy—Longarm thought his name was Tommy, Timmy, something like that—hadn't been told precisely where to find the visiting fireman, only that he was to go find the federal man and deliver the message.

Longarm sighed. Dammit, if a man was gonna have to be this miserable he at least should have the satisfaction of it paying off.

Too late for that, of course.

"Hey! You down there."

"Yes, sir?" The young deputy stared toward the ceiling in response to Longarm moving about now.

"Move that trash bin, will you? I don't want to come down on it when I drop." Longarm pulled aside the planks that covered the access hole to the attic, held Crockett's shotgun down for the deputy to take, and lowered himself until he was hanging by his hands, then bent his knees a little and dropped the remaining way to the floor. And to breathable air. Hot as it was inside the closed building it was still a hell of a lot more comfortable at floor level than it had been in that cursed attic.

"Give Marshal Crockett my thanks, son," Longarm said.

"Ain't you coming back to the jail with me? Boone said

something about you being expected for dinner.''

"No, but tell him thanks. Me, I got work to do.''

Feeling considerably let down, Longarm let himself out of the post office and made his way through a happy, moving crowd back in the direction of the ball field to rejoin the team.

Chapter 32

Douglas McWhortle snarled and snapped and otherwise expressed his contempt while he led Longarm well clear of the other ball players, then once they were out of hearing asked in a calm and pleasant tone of voice, "Did you do any good today?"

"Not hardly," Longarm complained, going on to explain the high hopes involving two good suspects who failed to show up. At which point the Capitals manager laughed, causing Longarm's eyebrows to kite upward.

"Your two suspects wouldn't have been named Joey Mascarelli and Jim Baxter, would they?"

"The first names are for sure the right ones," Longarm conceded, "but how the hell would you've known a thing like that?"

McWhortle chuckled and explained, "Those boys weren't in town to 'make a hit' like those girls thought. They were here to do some hitting. They came out while we were warming up for the game today and claimed they should have a try-out. Said they were the best batsmen ever to come out of . . . well, out of whatever one-horse township they come from. Said once we saw them bat we'd be pawing the ground ready to sign them up to a professional contract."

"Shit," Longarm mumbled. He glanced over toward the ball club but didn't see any strangers, so he asked the logical question.

"Of course they didn't make the team," McWhortle told

him, "though we gave them a chance to show us what they could do. After all, Jason needed to get warmed up anyway. The first kid showed he could hit a fastball down the middle well enough, so Jason gave him a shave."

When Longarm continued to look blank, obviously not knowing what the hell the manager meant by that, Mc-Whortle explained. "He threw one at the kid's jaw. Would have put a permanent dent in the left side of the boy's face if he hadn't ducked in time. Which nearly everyone does, by the way. But after that the kid was so gunshy he wouldn't stand within a bat's length of the plate and never so much as touched the horsehide again. The other boy, Baxter he was, could hit the fastball and wasn't so scared of chin music, but I doubt he'd ever seen a curve ball before. For sure he'd never tried to hit a professional quality curve. Once Jason started pitching those that boy was done hitting. So I thanked them for their interest and sent them back home. Wherever that is."

"I'd've been happier if they was the robbers instead of some farm boys wanting to run off and be famous," Longarm admitted.

"Next time," McWhortle said hopefully.

"Yeah."

"Got your things together?" the manager asked. "We leave on the westbound in forty-five minutes. Of course you're still under suspension, but if you ask real nice and agree to pay a fine by forfeiting one game's pay then I might let you back in the batting order this next game."

"Let's leave the suspension as it is," Longarm said. "I'll sulk off away from the team and try again to set up a trap for our boys if they show in . . . where are we going anyhow?"

"Town called Sorrel Branch."

"You do pick the big ones, don't you?"

"I do pick the ones so bored they pay for us to stop," McWhortle returned. Then, putting on a thoroughly pissed off expression, he commenced to rant and yell about pitcher Short's shortcomings.

A moment later the equipment boy Jerry showed up at Longarm's elbow to inquire about Longarm's gear, and Longarm realized that he and McWhortle were both back to playacting.

Longarm wiped the sweat off his neck and went about preparing to take another rattletrap train ride to nowhere.

Chapter 33

It was a long, slow grind to reach Sorrel Branch, partly because the narrow gauge P & P westbound stopped at every little whipstitch, either to handle freight or maybe so the engineer could take a leak, and partly because the farther west in Kansas they went, the fewer people there were who could come together and make a town.

By the time dawn and Sorrel Branch arrived, each at roughly the same time, Longarm figured they were about as far away from civilization as it was possible to get in the modern world.

Even so, Sorrel Branch was bigger than Longarm had expected. Which is to say that it was demonstrably bigger than a breadbox. But not much.

It consisted of a general mercantile, a smithy, a tool and harness shop, a barber/surgeon, two churches, assorted houses—most of them unimposing—and one lonely saloon.

"Yes, sir," Longarm mumbled half under his breath as he passed McWhortle on the patch of beaten earth and gravel that passed for a railroad depot, "you sure can pick 'em. Where's our hotel for tonight?"

"No hotel or boardinghouse here," the boss said loud enough for all to hear. "We play this afternoon and pull west again tonight."

Which precipitated a general round of groaning and grumbling. Two straight nights spent on the grimy upholstery of Plains and Pacific passenger coaches was considerably more than human flesh was intended to endure.

Yeah, Longarm thought, the life of the professional base-ball player was one glamorous son of a bitch, all right.

"All right, everybody. Breakfast is at the Catholic Church over there. Then we'll take some fielding practice and have our dinner courtesy of the Methodists in that church there. Or maybe it's the other way around. I'm not sure which church is which, but the Catholics will feed us breakfast and the Methodists dinner. Leave your things piled on the cart here. Jerry will stay and watch over everything. Short, you can take your meals with us but other than that stay out of my sight. No, better yet you can make yourself useful. When you're done eating you can bring a plate over to Jerry. All right now everybody, follow me." The manager set off at a brisk pace toward the nearer of the two churches. Whichever one it was and whether there was food waiting for them there or not.

Longarm held back and leaned on a suitcase that was damn near as battered and disreputable as his own. He reached into his pocket for a cheroot and lighted it. "Tell you what, kid," he said to the equipment boy, "You go ahead an' join the rest o' the team for breakfast, an' I'll eat when you're done. That'll be better than me tryin' to figure out what you like an' what you don't. I'm fine right here till you're done."

Jerry gave Longarm a look like he'd just been given a bright shiny toy for Christmas and ran to catch up with the team, which by now had gotten close enough to read the small sign beside the door of the church they'd been aiming for and had shifted their attention to the other church instead.

At least now he knew where to go for dinner, Longarm thought as he enjoyed the remarkably clean flavor of the cheroot he'd bought back in— What the hell was the name of that place anyhow? Already the whistlestop schedule was making the names and the memories meld into a single blur. Anyhow, the cigar was damned good. And surely that counted for something, didn't it? He leaned against the baggage cart with his eyes drooping closed and felt the heat of the coming day rise along with the sun.

Chapter 34

Damn, it was hot. Boring as hell, too. But then boring was the biggest part of being a peace officer. Which, come to think of it, was what a fellow wanted. The more boring things were the better they were going.

Still, there were times when it could get to a man. Waiting. All the damn time waiting for something stupid and wild and dangerous to happen. And then you earned your pay. Such as it was.

Longarm sighed and tossed away the butt of his fourth-or-so cigar of the day. He was hot, irritable, and wishing he could get this deal over and done with. Then maybe Billy would let him take a couple days off. He could take a train into the high country. Maybe go up to Fairplay. He knew some folks there who would put out the welcome mat . . . and perhaps offer some comforts even more hospitable than that. There was a lady named JaneAnn who . . .

Best to not be thinking about that, he told himself in no uncertain terms. Not when there was a job to be done. JaneAnn could be tended to after, not during. And for the time being . . .

He got up from the sidewalk bench where he'd been idling and ambled down the street toward the one and lonely saloon that the bustling burg of Sorrel Branch had to offer.

Longarm had long since learned there was no regular post office in the town. What there was was a set of pigeonholes and a tiny counter at the back of the mercantile.

Not much of a target for a sophisticated band of robbers but all the place had to offer. What Longarm figured to do was hang around and watch—there seemed no point in announcing his presence or his function, either one—while the townsfolk went off to watch the ball game.

If anybody wanted to break into the mercantile, good. Longarm would be willing to nab them.

As for the local law, well, there didn't seem to be any. Not that he could spot anyhow.

Which was a right fair excuse for a man to get off the hot and dusty street and step inside the cooler confines of a friendly saloon. Right? Damn straight.

He passed through a set of hanging fly beads and paused just inside the doorway for a moment to let his eyes adjust after the bright glare outdoors, then made his way to the bar. Which, he had to admit, was impressive.

The backbar was made of polished mahogany, carved into intricate patterns and set off with grinning gilt gargoyles and a set of mirrors and delicate latticework so nicely done that the many small mirrors were made to look like one very large one. Clever.

The place was crowded, the level of trade undoubtedly given a sharp boost by the promise of the baseball game that would take place later on. People would have come in from miles around, and every business in town was sure to benefit.

Longarm eased through the happy, chattering drinkers and found a spot within arm's length of the free lunch display. He snagged a pickled egg and a generous sized hunk of rat cheese and avoided a rebuke from the bartender by calling for a beer. Free lunch platters are for customers only, thank you.

"Anything else for you, mister?" the barman asked as he swept Longarm's nickel off the counter and into a pocket of his only slightly stained apron.

"Directions would help."

"Sure thing, friend. Kansas City is east, Denver is west, for Texas you go south." He smiled. "And there's not a damn thing of interest anyplace north of here. So what more do you want to know?"

Longarm laughed and said, "I was looking for the law hereabouts. Can't say that I found any."

"You aren't tall enough," the bartender said.

"Pardon me?"

"We aren't officially incorporated," the man explained. "Not that we'd have money enough to hire a marshal if we were. And not that we'd need a marshal if we could afford one. The last major crime we had around here was when Toby James snitched a pair of Widow Moore's unmentionables and ran them up the flagpole outside the blacksmith's place."

"Sounds pretty serious, all right," Longarm agreed.

"Yeah, we're hell for excitement around here. Count on it. Anyhow, we do have a county sheriff. See him once every other year when he comes around electioneering. And there's those who say we see him a mite too often at that. You ready for a refill on that, friend?"

Longarm nodded and dragged another nickel out of his pocket.

"If you really need a deputy you can likely find one at the county seat," the man said as he tilted a fresh mug beneath his tap and commenced drawing a second draft. "That's twenty-two and a half miles . . . more or less . . . due north from here."

Longarm grinned. "Due north."

"Ayuh."

"Not a thing of value north of here though," Longarm paraphrased.

"So some say." The bartender used a wooden paddle to knock the head off Longarm's beer and set the mug down, exchanging it for the nickel. "If you really need the help of a deputy, friend, we'll see what we can do."

"Not really," Longarm said, not particularly inclined to explain any further than that. He took a swallow of the fresh beer and wished it was cold. Some of the tonier saloons in Denver had taken to keeping their kegs on ice, which made a beer all the more welcome during the heat of summer. It was a damned shame the fad hadn't extended quite this far.

But then who knew where the nearest artificial ice making plant would be found or the nearest ice cutting and cold storage operation.

"In town for the ball game today?" the friendly barman asked as he wiped at an imaginary puddle on his bar.

"Not this son of a bitch," a new voice injected from off to Longarm's left.

Longarm froze, his mug poised just below chin level, and turned his eyes to see a sandy-haired man with a brushy mustache, coldly glittering dark eyes, and the butt of a large Remington revolver showing on his hip. The gun had received much use in the past, so much that there appeared to be no bluing left on the metal.

"The shit-eater is the law himself, Morris. Big man too. Calls himself Longarm. Like he's the long arm of the damn law, all of it rolled into one tall pile of garbage." The dark-eyed man glowered. "Isn't that right, Marshal Long Big Damn Deal Arm."

Longarm knew for certain sure that he never ever in his life saw the man before this very moment.

But he kinda doubted that the encounter was ended.

Not quite.

Slowly and carefully he set his mug down onto the bar and turned to face the belligerent fellow with the big .44 on his hip.

126

Chapter 35

It was really something to see. Like a first-class magician's practiced sleight of hand, the crowd around and behind the two men just kind of faded away. It was like ice melting at high speed. One moment there were dozens of laughing, cheerful, pleasant fellows standing around talking and drinking and looking forward to the afternoon's entertainment. And a blink later, maybe a blink and a half, there was a corridor of empty space stretching smack alongside of the bartop with only Longarm and the sandy-haired man left to face each other.

"Got paper out on you, do you?" Longarm asked conversationally.

"Not a scrap," the man told him.

"I shot down one of your kin then," Longarm suggested.

"Nope, nothing like that."

"Put a pal in jail?"

The fellow shook his head.

"Broke up a gang you was fond of."

"Huh uh."

This was becoming damn-all annoying, Longarm decided. Piss on the guy. "All right then, I screwed your wife. Your virgin sister . . . no, that couldn't of been it . . . you'd've screwed her first your own self, I'm sure. Okay, I screwed your mother and killed your father in the line of duty."

The gunman barked out a sound that Longarm assumed

127

was supposed to be a laugh, although it didn't sound over-much like one.

"Jeez, man, I must've done something to make you this hostile."

"Not a damn thing," the fellow assured him. "I just don't like smartass United States deputy marshals."

"Ah, that old reason. Now I feel better, knowin' what this here is all about. Mind if I ask you something else?"

"I reckon a man ought to be allowed a last question, same as a condemned man gets a last meal."

"Who the hell are you?" Longarm asked.

"William Beard. Does that mean anything to you?"

"Mister Beard, I hate to be such a complete disappointment to you, but I never in my life until this very minute heard anything about you, not even your name."

"My point exactly," Beard said.

"I beg your pardon?"

"Nobody has heard about me. I've killed eight men in standup fights, fair as fair can be, and no-damn-body has ever heard of me. I mean, it isn't fair, is it? Some fool in Dodge City kills two, three men and he's famous. Why? Because there are big city newspapermen who come to Dodge to write about stuff, and there's a local newspaper of their own that writes stories and sells them to the big papers back east and in Kansas City and the like. But here? Dammit, I could shoot down half the men in this jerkwater bar and there wouldn't be anybody ever hear about it outside this county. Might not pay attention in the county seat even if our good for nothing sheriff was busy getting laid that day. So what is a man to do, I ask you? It will take something big to be heard about here." Beard smiled. "And here you are. Famous. Well, more or less. Most famous lawman that ever stopped in Sorrel Branch, I can tell you that. You're a godsend, Long. I swear you are."

"Mister Beard, I'm always happy to accommodate a man, but dying for the sake of your reputation seems a mite more than is reasonable to ask. I hope it'll be all right with you if I demur."

"I wouldn't expect less, Longarm. Be a shallow victory indeed if you wasn't to fight back, now wouldn't it."

"Shallow indeed, Mister Beard. Uh, how d'you want t' go about this? Formal rules of the duel, maybe?"

Beard grinned. "And give you a choice of weapons, Mister Long? I think not. You see, I do know more than a little about you, and I suspect you would try to do something silly, like tell me you want to fight with sharpened tongue depressors or ass's jawbones or something like that. Something that would mock and make light of my triumph and my honor."

"I got to admit, Mister Beard, I always been fond o' the idea of a fight with the jawbones of some asses. I mean, it ain't reasonable that this don't happen all the time. You know? Asses an' assholes bein' so thick on the ground an' all."

"Don't try to make light of this, Mister Long. I do sincerely intend to kill you in fair and open combat. Please understand that."

"Oh, I do, Mister Beard. I surely do." Longarm pushed the situation just a bit by reaching—with his left hand, however—for his mug and taking a swallow of the tepid beer, his eyes locked on Beard above the rim of the glass.

"As for the rules, I propose that Morris here count backward from, say, ten. On the word Go we draw and fire. Nothing could be fairer than that, I daresay."

"He goes ten, nine, an' so on down t' one and then says Go?" Longarm asked.

"That's right. Would that be all right with you?"

"What if I'd like him t' count from twelve instead o' ten? Or from four. Would four be good for you?"

"Goddammit, Long, you're starting to piss me off now. You aren't taking this at all seriously."

"Sorry." Longarm shrugged, drank another sip and put

the mug down again. "I'll try an' get in the spirit o' things."

"Thank you."

"Looka-here," Longarm said. "If we're going t' do this we really oughta do it right. Honorable and aboveboard. You know what I mean?"

"I'm not sure that I do," Beard admitted.

"No funny business with choice of weapons, mind. I mean, we both are carrying our own favorites. Be kinda dumb to take up anything else. But except for that, well, there's something extra special honorable an' right about a proper duel. Especially the part where the two men stand back to back an' pace off a distance between them. Takes a perfectly honorable man t' turn his back on a fellow who's declared to kill him. Don't you agree?"

"I do, Mister Long. By God, I do. Thank you for understanding."

"I won't say it's my pleasure, Mister Beard, but I do understand."

"You would do that, then? You would stand with me back to back and pace off the distance while Morris counts our steps?"

"That I would, Mister Beard."

"Nobody could ever say a fight like that wasn't fair, could they?"

"No man alive could make a false claim like that, Mister Beard. The victor would be above reproach."

"I like it, Mister Long. Morris, you will count the paces for us. At the last number then we turn and fire at will. Is that the way you see it, Mister Long?"

"It is, Mister Beard."

Beard frowned and looked from one end of the bar to the other. "Ten is the traditional number of paces if I remember correctly, but I don't believe this room is big enough for us to take ten paces each."

"A point well taken, Mister Beard." Longarm looked

130

into the crowd, selecting at random from a sea—well, a good-sized pond then—of faces he'd never seen before.

Almost a sea of strangers, that is. The Austin Capitals' equipment boy was standing at the fringe of the onlookers. who, Longarm noticed, seemed even more numerous than they had been when this insanity commenced. Apparently the word was spreading and the gallery of spectators growing. Longarm hoped there were people still interested in the ball game afterward, although how could a mere baseball game compare with excellent drama—ahem—like this here.

"You," he said, pointing to a man of medium height and build. "Would you be so kind, sir, as to pace off the length of the room starting from that wall and crossing to that one?"

"Shit, yeah, why not?"

The man, a farmer judging by his clothes and by the baked and wrinkled skin at the back of his neck, took the request seriously. He positioned himself with his back firm against one wall and extended his left foot first, reaching out quite far with it and sonorously counting, "One," in a loud voice.

"Fourteen," he announced to one and all as he reached the far wall.

"Fourteen," Longarm repeated. "Seven paces each. But then it would be awkward if we were standing tight to the wall, don't you think? Would you agree to five paces each, Mister Beard?"

"I would, Mister Long. Five paces it will be. Is that all right with you, Morris?"

"Jesus, Will, are you sure you . . ."

"Don't provoke me, Morris. I intend to be here after the duel. Mister Long will not."

"You will, of course, allow me t' take a hand in my own defense before you reach that conclusion," Longarm injected.

"Your pardon, sir. I meant to imply no less." Beard bent over into a sort of a bow.

Jeez, Longarm thought, the idiot was really getting into the spirit of this French duel bullshit. Beard was acting stiff and formal and downright courtly all of a sudden.

"Right there for the starting point?" Longarm suggested, motioning toward a spot that looked like it was midway across the room.

"Perfect," Beard assured him.

"Back to back and guns in the holsters, is that it then?" Longarm asked. "Or d'you want to have the guns already in hand when we turn an' fire?"

"Oh, in the holsters, I should think. Don't you?"

"Much more sporting that way," Longarm agreed.

Beard smiled. "That's it then. It couldn't be better. And I have to thank you again, Mister Long. You honor me by standing with your back to mine. I know everyone will remember that part and talk about it for years to come. My biographers will write about it, too. I shall insist on that."

"Are we ready, Mister Beard? Aren't we supposed to share a cup before the combat?"

"Are we?"

"I think so."

"Morris. Would you please?"

The bartender complied with fresh mugs of beer. Beard quaffed his practically at a gulp. Longarm barely sipped at his. Around them the crowd pushed and shifted, closing in tighter and tighter to the lane left open for gunfire until it was almost a certainty that a bullet the slightest degree off target would do damage to the cheering section as well as to the combatants.

"Ready, Mister Long," Beard announced when his mug was empty.

"Ready, Mister Beard," Longarm assured him.

"Morris?"

"If you're sure . . ."

132

"Morris, please."

"All right then. Gentlemen, take your places."

Beard immediately turned around, presenting his back stiff and taut, his spine ramrod straight and his jaw firm.

Longarm nodded and moved up close behind him.

"I will count to five, gentlemen," Morris said in a voice loud enough for everyone in the place to hear. "You will take one pace forward with each number I count. When you hear me say five, but not a moment before, you are free to turn, draw and fire your pistols. If you are ready then . . ."

Chapter 36

"Are you ready, Mister Beard?"

"I . . . I . . . yes, I am."

"Are you ready, Mister Long?"

Instead of answering Longarm swung around, his Colt already in hand, and used the flat of the gun's butt to whack the beejabbers out of Beard, hitting him—hard—just above the nape of his neck.

Beard went down like a poleaxed shoat. It was probably as complete and clean a drop as Longarm ever did see.

"Hey!" someone in the crowd complained. "That wasn't fair."

The cry was taken up by others, a good half of the men crowded into the saloon bitching aloud now that there would be no blood spilled.

"You lied," another voice called out.

"Yeah, I sure as hell did, didn't I?" Longarm agreed calmly as he first relieved Beard of the burden of his Remington revolver, then dragged the limp body aside a few feet so he could prop Beard up against the bar.

"Will he be all right?" the bartender leaned over and asked.

"Should be. I think it's safe t' assume that he has a pretty hard head." Longarm frisked Beard while he had the chance but found no other weapons on him. Well, he hadn't expected any.

"You really weren't fair to him, you know."

Longarm looked at Morris the barman and shrugged,

feeling not the least lick of guilt for refusing to kill a man. "Guns ain't fair t' begin with, friend, an' the only object in a death scrap is t' win. Which maybe now Mister Beard will live long enough t' learn. An' that reminds me. Anybody here able t' back up his claim that he's killed eight men because I got to tell you I don't think he's ever before faced a grown man with a gun in his hand."

No one spoke. Finally a smallish fellow wearing bib overalls pushed toward the front edge of the crowd and said, "I don't know anything about that, but I can tell you that Will practices with that gun of his about every day. He spends hours and hours down in the gully that runs between our places, down there drawing and shooting, drawing and shooting. I've watched him, marshal, and I've never seen anything as quick as Will is with that gun of his. He's quicker than any snake I ever seen strike, and that's the truth."

By now Beard was commencing to stir as he came back to consciousness. Longarm hoped the fellow was listening.

"Quick noises or even quick an' accurate shooting ain't enough when it comes to the real thing," Longarm said. "An' for that there's no such thing as practice. The thing is different when the other fellow intends to shoot back. A man not only has to be good with his gun he has to have it in him to take the life of another human soul. Has to be willing to send a ball o' hot metal inta the flesh of another man an' take that man's life away from him. Not many can do that. Not near so many as believe they can."

"And Will Beard?"

"I hope he never finds out. Anyway, he won't learn it from me. Not today he won't."

"You gonna arrest him, marshal?"

"Naw, no point. I sure hell could o' course. Half a dozen charges I could lay against him, but I got better things t' do than haul him twenty-some miles north. As it is he's gonna be woozy and hurting for the next couple days after

135

a blow like the one I just gave him. Somebody . . . you there that's his neighbor maybe . . . somebody drag him home an' dump him into his bed. He got a wife or somebody t' tend him? No? Well then he'll just have to tough it out until he can walk without his knees turning t' rubber and his skull feeling like it's fixing to split apart. I'll let the rest of it be for now.''

Most of the men in the place still looked disappointed. But no one seemed inclined to volunteer as a replacement in the jousting lists with a United States deputy marshal.

Longarm looked about but did not see Jerry, the Capitals' equipment boy. Didn't see the beer he'd left on the bar either. There wasn't time enough for a fresh one. Not right now. He needed to find Jerry and have a word with him, make sure the boy understood that it wasn't to be nosed around about ''pitcher'' Chet Short's true identity.

After that, well, it was coming on toward lunchtime. Longarm figured to eat with the team and then find himself a good place where he could lie in wait for that gang of robbers in case this was his lucky day—and their bad one— and they tried to hit the Sorrel Branch post office safe.

Chapter 37

"Look, Jerry, I, uh, I enjoy your company an' appreciate your interest, but I got work to do." The clubfooted kid had been hanging around all big eyed and full of questions ever since the incident at the saloon. Longarm supposed he should be flattered and maybe he would have time enough to think so later, but for right now he was more interested in setting up an ambush for the robbery gang. And the only contribution young Jerry could possibly make would be to get in the way.

"Sure thing, marshal. I mean . . . Chet." The kid grinned and winked conspiratorially, sharing that momentous secret with the tall man who turned out to be so much more than he'd seemed.

"Just mind you don't let slip to anybody who I am, Jerry. Remember what you promised."

"I won't forget nothing that important, marshal. I won't even mention it to Mr. McWhortle."

Longarm wondered if he should reinforce that promise when it came to Nat Lewis, who was his only real suspect so far, then decided that to single out any one team member would only excite Jerry's curiosity all the further. Better to let things stand as they were than to add fuel to the kid's already blazing imagination.

"I'm counting on you, son."

"And if I can he'p you in any way."

"You have my word on it, Jerry. I'll come to you if and when I need any help with this investigation."

The boy beamed with childish pride. Childish. Jerry was probably seventeen or even older but he acted like a child in many ways and seemed, emotionally and perhaps mentally, younger than his age would indicate. Longarm felt sorry for him.

And immediately put him out of mind once Jerry backed away, assurances of secrecy pouring out of him as he did so, and went off down the street in the direction of the field where the ball game would soon be under way.

Longarm explored the crevasses between his teeth with a probing tongue tip and excavated a tiny scrap of pork loin that had been driving him nuts ever since lunch. He spat it out and in celebration lighted a fresh cheroot to help settle what had turned out to be an uncommonly good meal.

Now if the rest of the day went so well . . .

The makeshift ball field was only four blocks west of the mercantile-cum-post office where Longarm had posted himself. He could hear sporadic cheers—no doubt when the home team managed something good—and from time to time thought he could even detect the sharp crack of a pitched ball meeting a billet of fast moving wood. He almost wished he could see the game. Of course games are for children. Everyone knows that. But he was finding the essentially silly spectacle rather enjoyable for all its childishness. Fun, even. He hadn't expected that.

He heard—he was sure of it this time—an exceptionally loud crack swiftly followed by a roaring shout of approval from the several hundreds of people who'd shown up, and paid good money, to watch. Damn locals must've hit a homer. If they got one off Jason Hubbard, there would be some sulking and tantrums on the train tonight. Jason was a terrible loser and didn't mind who knew it.

Longarm shifted position. He was perched on the flat of an upended nail keg that had been discarded in the alley that ran behind the mercantile building. Longarm had dragged it behind a screening lump of tall weeds—the greenery was too ugly to have been deliberately planted, and anyway who would plant shrubbery in an alley—and was sitting there waiting.

It wasn't a bad place, but the iron-bound rim of the keg was cutting into the cheeks of his ass and threatening to put his whole hind end to sleep. And he couldn't stand upright and move around any because the weeds he was lurking behind weren't tall enough. Couldn't smoke here either lest that serve as a tell-all and give his position away. Just in case someone happened to be alert for signs of the law. Which he damn sure hoped would prove to be the case here.

He stifled a yawn.

Then came alert and bolt upright on the keg, the miseries in his butt forgotten as there was a flicker of movement down at the far end of the alley.

A hint of motion. Then nothing and then . . .

A scrawny white and tan bitch with her dugs hanging down to knee level came stepping into view and began sniffing through the alley trash in search of something edible.

Dammit.

Longarm shoved his Colt back into its holster—he hadn't consciously thought to draw the gun but had it in hand just the same—and once more allowed himself to slouch into a more comfortable position atop the miserable damned keg.

If only he could have himself a smoke . . .

Chapter 38

Longarm sprang to his feet as three—no, four now—dull reports marred the clamoring of the baseball crowd.

Gunshots. Two, then one, then a pause of several seconds and the fourth shot.

The sounds came from down the street to the west. From the ball field. Longarm was almost positive that was where the disturbance was.

He scowled. Dammit. *Damm* it!

Here he sat defending the post office, and some son of a bitch was down the street holding up the ticket booth.

Longarm ran along the side of the mercantile and burst out onto the main street of Sorrel Branch just in time to see three horsemen riding low on the necks of their horses come sweeping toward him from the direction of the ball field.

There wasn't a whole helluva lot of doubt that these were the boys he was interested in.

The flour sack masks they wore over their heads kinda gave them away. The sacks had red and black printing to advertise some brand of flour—Longarm was much too far away to read just what kind it was—and eye and mouth holes cut out. The masks were held in place by floppy hats jammed tight over them.

And the horsemen had revolvers in their hands.

They were riding fast but controlled and in fact seemed to be paying damned little attention to the street where Longarm had run into view.

At virtually the same time that he reached the street and saw them, the leader of the trio reached the cross street at the end of the block and turned to motion the others to follow as he reined his mount hard left into the side street.

Longarm had no time to aim and shoot before the last of them wheeled around the corner and out of sight. Cursing, Longarm started forward, then stopped again as the sound of flying hoofs once again seemed to be approaching.

But something did not seem right about it.

Then he realized. The riders were not on the next street over paralleling Main.

For some crazy reason the robbers were streaking through the alley behind the mercantile.

Longarm snarled and cursed his luck. If he'd stayed where he was to begin with they would have blundered right past him.

As it was, they were half a block away and. . . .

About the time he figured out what the hell was happening the first of the men galloped past the narrow opening Longarm had just raced through to reach the street. He caught a fleeting glimpse of the first rider and close behind him each of the others as they ran their horses through the alley.

There was a booming of gunshots, the sounds trapped and reverberating between the buildings, as the men fired at something—Longarm couldn't figure out what—back there in the alley.

He heard the shots and the tinkle of falling glass and then the hoofbeats faded as the riders reached the next cross street and turned north away from what little town there was to Sorrel Branch.

It was way the hell and gone too late for him to do anything now but Longarm couldn't help but run to the end of the block and look north toward the dust the robbers left behind.

The riders charged out of town and across a field of oat

stubble, then cut due east again just as they reached the screening line of crackwillow that grew beside a ditch to the north of town.

Damn them, Longarm thought. Damn them anyway.

Dispirited and grumpy as hell now, he shoved his Colt back into leather and started the long walk that would tell him how much the bastards got away with.

Damn them.

Chapter 39

"We're just about tapped out, boys," Douglas McWhortle announced to his ball players at the railway station late that afternoon. "That's twice we've had our pay snatched out from under us lately, and I'm frankly not sure if I have enough cash in hand to carry us. For sure there won't be any game pay handed out. We don't play again until Saturday so we won't be paid again until then. Whether we can make it or not depends on whether we can get credit at the boardinghouse in Jonesboro. If anyone wants to cut loose and find his way home on his own, well, I won't hold it against you."

There were long faces at that suggestion but no takers. But then probably no one had enough money for a train ticket home even if that was what he would want, Longarm suspected. The robbery of the gate receipts had made this a glum crowd indeed.

"At least our fare to Jonesboro is paid," McWhortle said on a slightly brighter note, "and the passage includes a box lunch for each of us. You won't go hungry tonight."

The team members filed silently onto the P and P passenger coach, leaving behind an equally solemn crowd in Sorrel Branch.

There was talk of getting a posse together, but with neither law nor organized leadership in the community that idea would likely remain in the talking stages. Regardless, it was already much too late to put anyone on the trail of the robbers. They already had several hours' headstart and soon it would be dark. By now the trio of gunmen—it was only dumb luck that kept anyone from being wounded . . . or worse—could be considered long gone.

"Psst!"

Longarm glanced over his shoulder as he was preparing to climb the steel steps into the rail car. Jerry, who should have been back in the baggage car, was standing there.

"Psst. Sir."

Longarm dropped back onto the platform and let Caleb Jones board ahead of him while Longarm made as if to light a cheroot and kind of accidentally moved closer to Jerry. "What is it, son?"

"Shouldn't you . . . I mean, aren't you going to *do* something about those awful people?"

"Like what?"

"Like . . . I don't know. I heard some of the men in town say they're putting a posse together. Shouldn't you take charge of that? I mean, you *are* a deputy marshal and all that."

"Which you are s'posed to forget all about, right?" Longarm said as he dipped the tip end of his cheroot into the flame of a lucifer.

"Well yes, but . . ."

"Thanks for the suggestion, son, but let me take care o' this."

"I just thought . . ."

"I know. It's all right."

"I heard somebody else say we won't be bothered by them robbers no more," Jerry put in this time, obviously unwilling to let go of such an exciting topic of discussion. And with a real life federal lawman at that. The kid might not be able to brag and bluster his secrets around the other members of the Capitals, but Longarm was another story.

"Why's that, son?"

"They said the robbers were seen heading east. We're going west and by a fast train. There's no way they could turn around and catch up with us again now."

"Even though we'll have three days in Jonesboro?" Longarm asked.

Jerry looked crestfallen. "I never thought . . . say, how fast can a horse run anyhow?"

"It ain't a question of how fast they are. A train can outrun a horse any time. It's a matter of how far a horse can travel one day after another."

"And to Jonesboro?"

Longarm thought about it a moment, then smiled and reached out to tousle Jerry's lank hair. "I reckon it's far enough we won't have to worry about seeing the gang there in just three days. They might come after us at the next stop or the one after that, I wouldn't know. But I expect it's fair to say we won't have t' worry about them in Jonesboro."

Jerry looked considerably relieved after that assurance. "Thanks, Marshal."

"Huh uh. I'm Chet. Remember?"

"Yes, sir. I mean . . . Chet." The kid grinned and trotted—well, hippety-hopped would be more like it but it was what passed for a trot on his bum foot—back down the train in the direction of the baggage car where he always was stuck watching over the team's things.

"Boooo-ard!" the conductor called as coupling pins crashed and steam whistles shrilled. The P and P train lurched and jerked into motion.

Longarm had to hustle to make it onto the train before the clattering monster built up speed.

Chapter 40

"Make yourselves comfortable," McWhortle told his red-eyed and weary collection of baseball warriors. "We'll be here until after the game Saturday. Plenty of time for you to sleep."

"What's today?" one of the boys asked. Which was not really the dumb question it might have sounded. On a trip like this the days as well as the towns all blended into one, and if Longarm hadn't been paying close attention he likely would not have known either.

"Thursday," McWhortle answered in a matter-of-fact tone. "One more thing before you make a run for the beds. I've already talked to Mrs. Mosely who runs the place. She knows we're broke and she's willing to work with us. But be nice to her, will you? No shenanigans, hear? No water fights in the hallway and no food fights at table. And don't be wasting food, all right? The lady will probably go light on the meat and other expensive stuff when she feeds us. Don't any of you say anything to her about it. She's treating us right. I want you all to act like," he grinned, "little gentlemen. All right?"

The ball players grumbled a bit but not too much. Longarm thought most of them would probably go along with the deal and put on their best behavior, at least until the team's bills were paid and they could act like their own ornery, immature selves again.

"That's it then," McWhortle said. "Everybody try and get some rest and I'll see you at lunch. Oh, yeah. One more thing. We're doubling up in the rooms to save money. No more privacy, so mind you don't step on each other."

That brought a loud chorus of groans and mumbles, but by then the manager had ducked inside and was already out of sight and hearing alike. The rest of the bunch trailed unhappily indoors except for Longarm who hung back on the porch fingering a smoke.

"Aren't you coming . . . Chet?" Jerry asked.

"Be right along, kid. I wanta stretch my legs after all night on those padded damn benches. I'll take a stroll while I finish this cigar an' join you inside."

Jerry grinned. "You're already too late to get a good choice of roomies."

"That don't matter t' me."

"You wouldn't . . . I mean . . . you wouldn't consider bunking in with me, would you?"

"Sure, why not."

Jerry grinned big as a shit-eating possum hunkered down over a fresh pile of bear doo. "You mean that?"

" 'Course I do."

"All right then, Mar . . . I mean, Chet. You go on and enjoy your walk. I'll have your things all laid out in our room when you get back. And . . . and you can have the best bed too. I promise."

Damned if Longarm didn't think he meant it. "Thanks, Jerry." He turned and wandered away but headed not immediately down the street but around to the back of the boardinghouse first. He hadn't had a chance yet this morning for the pleasure of a leisurely crap.

First things first, after all.

Chapter 41

Longarm rinsed his hands and bent low over the basin, plunging his face into the chill water and washing some of the cobwebs out of his brain. Or so it felt like anyway. Two nights of trying to sleep on jolting trains can do that to a fellow.

He rubbed his eyes and behind his ears and scrubbed some at the bristling beard stubble that darkened his cheeks. It wouldn't hurt to find a barber and treat himself to a good shave, he thought. Either that or risk cutting his own damn throat if he tried to do the job on his own.

Eyes closed against the sting of the soap residue floating in the wash water he straightened up and groped along the wall in the direction where he thought he remembered the age-gray towel hanging.

"Is this what you're looking for?" The voice was feminine and soft. At the same time the woman spoke Longarm felt the coarse fabric of the flour sack towel being placed in his hand.

The first order of business was to wipe his face so he could open his eyes and . . .

Oh my, that was effort well spent.

The girl was pretty. Well, mostly. She had a complexion like fresh cream, eyelashes as long and curly as those on a Jersey calf, eyes as blue and sparkling as . . . as something mighty damned blue and sparkly whatever such would be, and tits big enough to suckle a troop of cavalry with milk left over.

She also had a jaw that would have looked in dainty proportion had it been slung from the face of a small moose.

But hell, with knockers like those feather-pillows of hers a girl could be forgiven a few minor faults.

"Thank you, Miss . . . ?"

"You can call me Fancy," the girl said, and giggled.

Longarm was commencing to suspect that something was afoot here.

"Fancy is the name and it's fancy that you are," he said with a deep bow. "My name is Chet."

"Could you help me with something, Chet?" she asked.

"If it is within my power, Fancy, the favor is surely yours."

"My, you do talk nice, Chet."

"Not nearly so nice as you look, m'dear."

She giggled again. "Could you come along and lift something down for me?"

"My pleasure, pretty girl." He quickly dabbed the towel over his neck and behind his ears, then put it back onto the hook where the girl found it.

"This way, please." She started off toward the back of the lot where the boardinghouse was situated, and for a moment Longarm thought she was taking him to the outhouse where he'd just completed his morning's business.

Instead, though, Fancy led him through some scraggly shrubbery and on to a building that might originally have been intended as a carriage house. It was too big to be considered a shed, he decided, but was much too small to be a barn. A storage building of some sort now, he concluded. It had seen better days.

"In here, Chet."

Fancy pulled one of the broad double doors open, ancient hinges offering a squeal of protest at that intrusion, and disappeared into a gloomy interior that was highlighted here and there by dust motes flitting through slender beams of

149

light that crept through gaps in the curling roof shingles.

Longarm blinked, his eyes not yet adjusted to the darkness as he stepped in behind the girl. "Where . . . ?"

And then he knew right good and well where she'd gotten to.

Pressed tight against him, that's where she was. And if he didn't take care she was apt to suck the breath clean out of his lungs.

Fancy didn't seem to know a whole hell of a lot about the fine arts and sciences of the kiss. But she was for sure willing to do what little she knew how with gusto. Mucho gusto.

Chapter 42

Ah yes, the delicate and lovely nuances of genteel court-ship. Fancy's version of courtship was on the same order of things as illustrating the proper techniques of the social call with Sherman's visit to Atlanta. Flames and all. Damn, but the girl was hot.

He meant that literally, actually. The day was another scorcher and Fancy was sticky with sweat. Smelled of yesterday's sweat, too. And maybe a somewhat more extensive collection as well although he'd rather not have to think about that at the moment.

There were, ahem, other matters to consider just now.

Like how to get those damned buttons   there, that was better.

He got the top of her dress open while Fancy was busy with his fly. It'd seemed something of a race that turned out to be a tie. Not that there was any harm in that.

She was wearing a thin chemise under the dress. That posed no problem for a man of Longarm's experience. Especially as the material of the chemise was old and often washed. The pale cloth kind of disintegrated under his touch—he swore he hadn't jerked or pulled or *tried* to tear it open—and her tits popped out into full, glorious view.

More than a mouthful? These melons were more than a half gallon. Each. An incautious man might could smother himself to death if Fancy leaned down over him. Which might not be the very worst possible way a man could happen to die. But still. . . .

She had a little heat rash underneath the sag of those bazooms and would have benefited from some powder. But he wasn't complaining. He bent down and gobbled in a mouthful of nipple on her left one while he gave the other a hearty squeeze, and Fancy went to moaning like she was already in ecstasy.

"Oh God, honey, do me, do me quick, sweetie." She snatched the hem of her dress waist high, the wonders thus revealed being instantly and fully on display as she hadn't bothered with pantaloons when she dressed earlier. A shy girl, Fancy. Demure and withdrawn. Yeah. "Do me, honey."

She waggled her butt, which set her tits to flopping, and Longarm bore down all the harder to keep control of the one he was trying to suck. He didn't know but what he maybe should set his spurs and hang on or else back away fast so as not to get slapped silly by all the meat that was being slung. He settled for taking a firm hold with his teeth and squeezing even harder on the other one.

Fancy groaned and wriggled and subtly indicated that, uh huh, she liked that just fine. "Harder, baby, harder," she moaned. "Bite it, honey. Hard."

He complied, hoping he wasn't commencing to draw blood, and Fancy let out a loose, satisfied little squeal and kind of shivered some. He would almost have sworn that she reached a climax just then.

He moved over to the other tit and bit it too, and Fancy went so far out of it that her knees buckled and for about half a second there he thought he was gonna have to support her full weight on the nipple he was gnawing. Fortunately she got her balance back after that brief scare and continued to grope and grasp him.

She'd been having trouble getting his cock out where she could enjoy it but now she ripped the thing out of its confines—damned lucky for him he wasn't fully hard yet so there was still some bend and give to the poor thing;

otherwise he'd have had to set the break and put it in a splint and then where the hell would he have been—and got a good look at it for the first time.

The girl cackled and turned loose of him long enough to clap her hands in glee. "Sweetheart, I think I'm in love."

"I'll take that as a compliment," he told her.

"Take whatever you want, honey, just so I can take that big beautiful thing inside me."

Uh huh. Shy. He hoped she'd outgrow that trait someday.

Fancy grabbed him by the nuts—she only wanted to fondle him, but she was such a vigorous broad that he was gun-shy and would have leaped away from her except she was too quick for him. If he'd pulled back once she had hold of him, he likely would have left his cojones behind, and she dragged him with her as she backed up in search of something to lean against.

She backed into a dirt crusted and rotting barrel and leaned against it, spreading her ample thighs and drawing Longarm right onto—and into—the wet heat of her sweating body.

Ready? She couldn't have been any more slick and greasy if she'd been bathing in a tub of snot. He slid inside easy as dunking a biscuit in gravy and mightn't have been sure he was in her if it hadn't been for the heat that surrounded him.

Ready? He hadn't more than bumped his belly tight to hers than Fancy went to shuddering and huffing and turning all red in the face. She wiggled and moaned and the lips of her pussy contracted so hard that he could actually feel her around him. The girl was just plain big. Loose and sloppy and big enough so that even he, big as he was, had room left over.

Longarm knew that while Fancy might be having a helluva lot of fun this way he wasn't likely to get much out of it. Not like this. He pulled out and turned her around, giving her a little push so that she leaned facedown over the top of the ancient barrel.

"You want me in the ass, sweetie? You go right ahead, honey. I like it there too."

Interesting, he supposed, and a generous offer. But not exactly what he had in mind.

"Pull your legs together."

"Make me," she demanded.

He didn't understand what she wanted at first. Then did. What the hell, it was her quirk not his. He slapped her butt a couple times, harder than he really wanted if not so hard as she would have liked, and Fancy climaxed again under this tender treatment. "Now put your legs close together," he repeated.

This time Fancy did what she was told—hell, if she got balky he might refuse to spank her again—and Longarm stepped up behind her broad ass.

This time when he slid the meat into her locker she was tight enough that he could enjoy being there.

And truth to tell there was something about Fancy that had him just damn near as hot as she'd been.

He stirred it around a few times and soon felt the swift rise of intense pressure building deep in his balls and flowing up into his cock.

He held back, trying to contain it, but it was like trying to hold back the spring floods. Just couldn't be done.

When he came it was a flood sure enough. He pumped fluid enough to make a fire engine proud, and while he was doing that Fancy came again, too.

Longarm's knees went weak and his eyes crossed—well, they almost felt like they *might* have—and he had sudden visions of soft beds that didn't rock and jolt along a bunch of damned railroad tracks and long hours of uninterrupted sleep and things like that.

But then he was a United States deputy marshal here trying to do his duty.

154

Right.

He swayed backward, letting his limp, wet pecker flop out into the cooling air.

"Lawd'a'mercy, sweetheart," Fancy said. Or something like that.

"Yeah," Longarm agreed. He yawned and patted Fancy on the butt, which did not get a rise out of her this time. He supposed she must've been pretty well spent by now too, though.

"Excuse me, honey," he told her, "but I gotta go see a man about a horse."

Fancy made a face at him but didn't object when Longarm went to tucking and buttoning himself into outward respectability again.

"Any time you want to talk some more . . . " she offered.

Longarm smiled and winked at her and leaned forward to plant a chaste, brotherly little kiss on the tip of her nose.

Then he turned and got the hell out of the close confinement of the old carriage house. Damn girl smelled like a goat, he swore she did.

Chapter 43

At some point not long before daybreak the P & P train had crossed the state line, carrying the baseball club out of flat, drab, and dreary Kansas and into a piece of Colorado that was . . . every damn bit as flat and drab and dreary as it'd been back in Kansas.

But at least this was *familiarly* flat, drab and dreary. Hell, it seemed practically like home after being stuck in Kansas so long. Not that Longarm had anything against Kansas. Far from it. But Colorado was home territory and he was pleased to be back.

He stood in the middle of the main street of Jonesboro—he didn't exactly have to fret about being run over by the crush of onrushing traffic; at the moment the only thing he could see moving at ground level was a stray cat that emerged from an alley, took one look around and quickly retreated back into the shade of the alley it just came from—and took a deep drag on a cheroot while he peered around.

He'd been in Jonesboro before. Twice if he remembered correctly. And the truth was that it had grown some since the last he saw it.

There still wasn't a tree to be found for fifteen or twenty miles in any direction, but here lately a forest seemed to've been growing anyway.

Windmills. The country had become of a sudden over-grown with brand-new windmills, each one of them busily pumping water into newly dug irrigation ditches. Jonesboro and environs was fast becoming farm country whereas the last time Longarm looked it had been devoted mostly to small-parcel livestock raising, like chickens, pigs, goats, and some sheep raised on a small scale.

Not now. Now everything around had been plowed, disked, dragged, and planted. The place would've been a vegetarian's version of heaven, he was sure.

And somewhere in the unseen distance there was a salesman for the Aeromotor Company who surely must have a permanent smile stitched into both corners of his mouth. The man's commissions from selling all these windmills would probably keep him in whiskey and women for the rest of his days, long may they be.

Likely too the P and P investors were excited. If only cautiously so. The last he'd heard the P and P had completed track only as far as Lamar, or maybe it was LaJunta, he couldn't remember which, before they called a "temporary" stop to the construction. Temporary, that is, until they found enough money to build on the rest of the way west to Trinidad where they hoped to connect with General Palmer's Denver and Rio Grande line and put the narrow gauge Plains and Pacific into a profitable situation.

This newfound growth in farming along the P and P route might be just what they needed. Or it as easily could be a pipe dream that would break a thousand backs and twice that many hearts when the wells ran dry or the locusts came or some other damn thing ruined the farmers who invested their hopes in this dry and unforgiving land.

Longarm wished them luck. And was damned glad that he wasn't one of them.

He finished his cigar, then ambled off down the street toward a saloon he remembered as being a right nice place to visit.

A drink would help to settle his stomach, he decided, and maybe as well help him to forget how scorching hot the day was becoming.

157

After that, well, he would poke around a mite, then go back to the boardinghouse and join the rest of the Capitals in catching up on some of that sleep he'd been missing the past couple nights courtesy of the Plains and Pacific.

Chapter 44

"Chet. Mr. Short. Wake up, sir, it's time to go down to supper."

Longarm came awake with a groan and a curse. Jerry, his ever eager, always anxious roommate was leaning over him. Longarm gave the kid a scowl to tell him how welcome this wake-up call was.

He sat upright on the edge of the lumpy, boardinghouse bed and made a sour face, which wasn't a patch on how sour the inside of his mouth tasted. The slime on his tongue tasted kind of like how cow slobbers look.

Worse, his head was pounding and felt like it had been packed in sand.

What was it about trying to sleep in daylight that so often made the cure seem less desirable than the original fatigue. He should have stayed awake through the afternoon. Of course now was a fine time to think about that.

"Are you coming, sir?"

"Yeah, yeah, leave me be, dammit." Longarm tried to rub some of the sting out of his eyes although they felt like they needed more than a light massage, they felt like they needed to be taken out and thoroughly washed. Put them into a basin of soapy water and scrub them clean, maybe that would take some of the misery off them.

On that cheery thought he climbed onto his hind legs and stumbled over to the washstand where the thunder mug was stored underneath. He pissed in the porcelain mug. It was just too damned far to contemplate going out back right

159

now. Besides, Fancy might be hanging around out there, lurking in ambush for the next poor SOB of a ball player to step outside. Longarm was in no humor for another piece of that. Later, maybe. Not right now.

"Are you all right, sir?"

"Yeah, sure," Longarm lied.

"Is there anything I can do to help you?" Jerry offered.

"No, there . . . wait a minute. You serious about that?"

"Yes, sir, just as serious as I know how."

"I tell you what then." Longarm plucked his coat out of the wardrobe and fumbled inside it for a cheroot and some matches. "Tell you what. I'm not feeling so good right now. Would you kinda keep an eye on one of the boys and tell me if he tries to slip out by himself this evening?"

The equipment boy lit up like Longarm had just ignited a set of candles inside his skull, like he was a living, breathing jack-o'-lantern. "You mean one of our own players is a suspect?" Jerry asked with so much excitement it was all he could do to form the words.

"I wouldn't go so far as t' say he's a suspect, exactly. It's just that I got a few questions I'd like t' see answered. You know what I mean?"

"Whatever you say, marshal." Jerry grinned and corrected himself. "I mean, Chet." The boy chuckled and— Longarm saw him do it and would have sworn to it in a court of law—actually, by-God rubbed his hands together in anticipation of this great excitement. "Who is it, sir? Who do you want me to watch for you?"

"You won't tell another soul? Swear to God you won't?"

"No one, marshal. I promise."

Longarm hesitated only long enough to get his cheroot alight, then lowered his voice to a conspiratorial whisper. "It's Nat Lewis, son. I want you to let me know if Nat tries to sneak out alone t'night."

160

Jerry looked purely fit to bust with the prospect of spying on a teammate before him. Longarm wasn't sure he had ever seen anyone quite so happy before. About anything.

"Sir?"

"Yeah, kid."

"We better go down now or we'll miss supper. And, sir?"

"Uh huh?"

"Don't you worry about what you asked me to do, sir. I won't let you down. I promise that I won't."

"Why, I trust you to that, son, or I wouldn't have asked you t' begin with."

Jerry beamed with joy and pride. He practically floated down the staircase to the dining room below. Longarm clumped along at a considerably more sedate pace.

The whole team was gathered there for a meal that was long on starches and gravy but short when it came to actual meat. Still, it was hot and filling and there was plenty of it. Afterward most of the men drifted into the parlor where they broke up into small groups, most of them centered around nucleuses of cards and coins.

Longarm got into a penny ante game of stud with the pitching staff.

He had no idea what Nat Lewis and Jerry were up to and took some care not to go looking around for either one of them.

Chapter 45

"Psst! Sir. Mr. Short."

Longarm looked up to see Jerry standing at the sliding double doors that led out to the entry hall and vestibule. The boy was hissing and beckoning for all he was worth. He might as well have waved a signal lantern and fired off some flares, but what the hell. Nobody cared anyway.

"I'm out. Do me a favor, Dennis?"

"Sure."

"Cash these out for me, please. I got an urgent call o' nature to see to."

"Sure, whatever you say." The young pitcher pulled Longarm's pile of pennies in front of him and grinned. "Now I can really run the pots up on these guys."

Longarm left the table and grabbed his Stetson off the elk horn rack on his way out to join Jerry.

"It's Nat Lewis, sir. He went out back like he was going to the shitter but he never. Instead he looked around . . . I was real careful that he couldn't see me watching after him . . . and took off into town. I didn't know what I should do then, sir. I mean, should I run back in to tell you and miss seeing where Nat went or should I follow after him. I decided to follow and see where he was going then come back for you. Is that all right, sir? Did I do good?"

"You did just fine, Jerry."

The boy beamed and led the way outside and down the street in the direction of downtown Jonesboro, Longarm having to shorten his strides to keep from overrunning the hippety-hop gait of the youngster with the clubfoot.

"Back in there it is, sir," he said once they were on Main next to Berman's Pharmacy. "He went down this alley here and knocked on a door. I waited long enough to overhear that much, then I hurried on back to get you."

"You did fine, Jerry. Couldn't have been any better."

"Thanks."

"Wait for me here on the street now."

"You don't want me to come with you, sir?"

Longarm didn't want Jerry getting in the way in a dark alley. Didn't particularly want to hurt his feelings either. "What I need is for you to stay here so no one can sneak up behind me. I'll feel better if I know there's someone watching my back, see."

"Oh. Right." Jerry grinned, obviously pleased to have such an important part in the continuation of this mission. "I won't let anybody come up behind you."

"If anything happens, son, don't try and fight. Just call out the warning and scoot out of sight."

"But you . . ."

"I'll be fine. Really. You ready now?"

"Yes, sir. I'm behind you. You can count on me, sir."

"Okay, but remember to keep your eyes on the street, not down the alley here. You won't be able to help if you're watching me instead of what's going on around us."

"I never thought of that." Jerry turned his back—reluctantly—on the alley and gave his attention to the completely empty city street.

For his part, Longarm simply sauntered down the middle of the alley. He could see lamp light in a window toward the back of the pharmacy and suspected that was where he would find Nat Lewis.

Longarm reached the window and had to go on tiptoes to see through the dirt-grimed panes of old, inferior glass. The poor quality of glass made everything inside appear wavy and slightly out of true, as if trying to look at

163

something on the bed of a fast-moving stream, but the light inside was good and the visibility sufficient for Longarm's purposes.

Lewis was in there all right, along with a young man Longarm had never seen before. The local fellow wore a white linen smock and white cotton gloves, sleeve garters and an eye shade. He was bent over a small table doing something that Longarm could not see while Nat Lewis paced back and forth nearby.

Whatever arrangement was being made here it wasn't quite yet concluded, that was obvious.

After a minute or so the man in white stood, leaning backward and pressing a hand into the small of his back as if to try and alleviate a pain there. He said something to Lewis and picked up the thing he'd been working with, which turned out to be a small mortar and pestle. Longarm could see them clearly now that the man—pharmacist? likely—was out of the way.

Lewis bobbed his head in response to whatever it was the local said, then reached into his pants pocket. He pulled out a thin sheaf of folded paper. Money, Longarm thought, although the poor visibility would not let him see that for certain sure, and handed it to the man in the white smock. The local took a careful look at the currency he'd been given—Longarm confirmed what it was when the fellow counted it—and pushed the bills into his pocket, then picked up the pestle and dumped something from it into an envelope which he handed to Lewis.

The ball player practically ripped the envelope open again in his haste to reach the contents. He pulled out a pinch of the powder and put the substance inside his mouth, pushing it into his cheek the way a man will sometimes use tobacco snuff, although Longarm was fairly sure that a body wouldn't go to a pharmacist for anything so simple as ordinary snuff.

On the other hand . . .

Longarm went over to the alley door and was waiting there when Nat Lewis stepped outside with his precious envelope in hand.

It didn't really matter to Longarm what it was that Lewis was up to here. Whatever it was it had nothing to do with post office robberies. Still, he was mildly curious.

"H'lo, Nat."

The outfielder acted like he would have come clean out of his skin if it hadn't been firmly closed on all sides. "Short. Jesus, man, what are you doing here?"

"I, uh, was looking for something else and couldn't help but notice your little transaction in there. Mind telling me what it was about?"

"It's . . . nothing. Really."

"Nothing, Nat? It's important enough for you to hide it from the rest of the team."

"I just . . . nothing, dammit. Leave me alone, Short. Just leave me be about this."

"I dunno, Nat. It kinda looks like the sort of thing as ought to be discussed with McWhortle."

"God, Short, you son of a bitch. You'd tell, wouldn't you? Don't. I'm begging you. You want money? Is that it? I . . . I don't have much left. When we get paid again maybe I can . . ."

"I don't want your money, Lewis. I just want you to tell me what it is you're doing. I mean, I saw you on the train one time taking delivery of something . . . or passing something along, I couldn't tell which . . . and now this. What is it that you're up to, Lewis?"

"I just . . . it isn't anything illegal, Short."

"Then why are you trying to hide it?"

"It's Douglas. He's dead set against . . . he'd kick me off the team if he found out, Short. I'd be ruined, my whole career shattered."

"For what, Lewis?"

"It's only coca powder. It's perfectly legal, you know. It doesn't harm anything, and it . . . it kind of helps."

"I see," Longarm said. And of course he did. The powdered coca was entirely legal just as Nat Lewis said. It was legal and it was cheap and it was used by many as a pick-me-up when they were tired or wanted a little boost of quick energy. Unfortunately the stuff could also be addictive and could lead, or so some claimed, to serious health consequences. Certainly it could affect one's judgment. Those likely were the reasons Douglas McWhortle would not want any of his players using the commonly available stuff.

Nat Lewis, it seemed, was already addicted beyond McWhortle's—or his own—ability to control.

The pharmacist must have overheard the voices outside his door because now he appeared there, this time without the smock and gloves. "Is everything all right out here?"

"Yes. No problem," Longarm assured him.

"You are sure?"

"Really," Lewis said.

"Good night then." The pharmacist closed the door and rather loudly locked and chained it.

"Short," Lewis said, his voice pleading. "You won't . . ."

Longarm sighed. "No, Lewis. I reckon I won't say nothing to McWhortle 'bout this. But I think . . . no, never mind. You don't want advice from me, I'm sure."

"Thank you, Chet. Thank you. You won't regret it. I promise."

The teammates left the alley in silence and proceeded back to the boardinghouse without speaking again.

There was no sign of Jerry on the street, Longarm noticed.

But then obviously the kid would have overheard everything that took place in the alley. No point in mentioning that to Lewis, though.

Two more days, Longarm thought. Two days and the Capitals would meet the Jonesboro nine.

And this game should not be marred by the presence of robbers. That was what he'd assured Jerry when the kid pressed him on the subject.

After that, well, after that they would just have to wait and see what happened, wouldn't they?

Chapter 46

The morning of game day Longarm crawled unwilling into his baseball outfit. He managed to refrain from sniveling and whining about it, but he did snarl and spit just a little.

"Something wrong, Marshal?" his roommate asked.

"Flannel at this time o' year, that's what's wrong." It wasn't yet midmorning and already the sweat was pouring off him by the bucketful. And that was indoors. In the fierce glare of the sunshine this afternoon it was bound to be unbearable. "How come you never complain, kid? Surely you get as hot and miserable as the rest of us."

"Oh, I don't mind the heat so much," Jerry admitted. "It's worth being hot to be able to wear a fine uniform like this. Can I ask you something?"

"Sure, go ahead."

"When you're out there on the field playing and all those pretty girls are cheering and then later they come up to you and . . . well, they do things with you . . . you know the sort of things I mean . . . is it, well, is it as grand as it looks?"

"I'm not sure I know what you mean, Jerry."

"I mean . . . those girls falling all over you and the other players . . . is it really, really neat?"

"I suppose so. Hadn't given it much thought, actually, but I s'pose you could call it neat."

Jerry blushed, then rushed on quick before he lost his courage. "You don't have to pay them or . . . or anything?"

"Hell no, kid. Girls like that, they're easy. They'd sleep with anybody."

The equipment boy looked sad. "Not everybody," he said.

Longarm glanced down toward the kid's twisted foot, then paid attention to Jerry's boyish but rather homely features and complexion. "Your time will come," he said.

Jerry brightened a little. Or pretended to. "Sure it will, marshal. One of these days I'll be rich. Maybe even famous, sort of. Then all the girls will want to be with me. Even more than with guys like you and the players. You wait and see. It will happen, sir."

"I believe you, Jerry. I bet it really will happen that way for you." It was a lie. But not a bad sort of lie.

"Can I ask you something else?"

"Sure, anything."

"You said you don't expect those robbers to be here in Jonesboro. Does that mean you'll be playing today?"

"I'll play if the manager wants me to."

"But you'll be there with us at the ball field, is that right?"

"All day long," Longarm assured him, checking to make sure all his buttons were buttoned and all the tail ends tucked in. Damn but he would be glad when he didn't have to wear this clown suit any longer.

"If there's anything you need, sir, or anything I can do."

"I know I can count on you to be close by, Jerry. In fact, I am counting on that."

"Yes, sir. Thank you, sir."

Longarm gave his gunbelt and Colt a looking over, but there was no help for it. Those particular items would be distinctly out of place in conjunction with a baseball uniform.

"You want me to carry those for you, marshal? Just in case, like? I could hide them on my cart. In the bat bag or better yet I could put them in my first aid box. It wouldn't be no trouble."

"Thanks, Jerry, but I won't need them. Not today."

Carefully he rolled the belt, gun, and holster into a compact bundle and stowed them away in his carpetbag.

"I'm ready to go now if you are, marshal."

"Let's go do it, son."

Chapter 47

To Longarm's immense relief the manager did not want
Longarm to start in right field. It was hot enough sitting on
the bench along the third base line. It would have been even
worse if he had to be running around out in the damned
field.

"Stay ready though, Short. I expect to need you to hit
for me later on."

"Is there somethin' I don't know about? How can you
tell before the game even starts that you'll be needin' a
punch hitter?"

"The term is pinch, not punch. And I'm anticipating it
because as you may not have noticed, it's a very hot day
today. The pitchers especially will be feeling that. I'll start
Jason Hubbard, but later on I'll want to put in Dennis Pyle
and possibly will replace him later, too. When I think it's
time to make the move, see, I'll wait until it's Jason's turn
to bat, then put you in long enough for that one at-bat. A
matter of simple strategy you see, not collusion."

"Damn. I guess maybe there's reasons for all the stuff
that goes on on that field, huh?"

McWhortle smiled. "Sometimes. Not always."

"Let me know when you want me t' hit," Longarm said.

"Relax. I won't need you for a spell."

"Thanks." Longarm looked rather longingly toward a
tent—the shade was reason enough to yearn for it—where
an enterprising soul was selling lemonade, apple cider or
beer, fifteen cents a glass for whichever one you chose.

171

Expensive, Longarm thought, but worth it.

"Go ahead," McWhortle told him. "Just don't dip too heavy into the beer if that's your pleasure."

"Lend me a dollar?" Longarm asked. "I didn't pack my wallet in these tight britches."

McWhortle forked over, and Longarm made for the refreshment tent.

He wasn't more than into the shade of the canvas canopy when he ran into a friend. Sort of.

"Ma'am," he said, reaching up to touch the brim of his Stetson only to realize too late that he was instead wearing that ridiculous, floppy baseball cap. Better to tip that than be rude, though. He removed it and smiled at the girl he knew as Fancy—which surely was not her right name—and at the much prettier lass who was with her.

"Geraldine, this is Mr. Short." Huh. She must've been asking after him then. They hadn't bothered with much in the way of introductions the last he saw Fancy. "Mr. Short, this is Miss Flowers."

"And pretty as a flower you are too, miss," Longarm said politely. It was not a lie. Geraldine was blonde and lovely, with a shapely figure and a dimpled smile. He couldn't help wondering if Geraldine Flowers had the same habits as Fancy did when it came to being, uh, hospitable to visiting baseball players.

Not that he could come right out and ask.

"May I offer you ladies a beverage?" Longarm asked.

"Cider for me, please," Fancy said. "A lemonade would be lovely," Geraldine added.

"I'll be with you in a moment."

The girls moved out of the crowd to the fringe of shade on the far side of the canopy while Longarm pushed his way through the sweating, smelling press of humanity to fetch the drinks. It was a good thing McWhortle had given him more than the price of a single beer, bless that man's heart.

Out on the field the game was already in progress. Both young ladies seemed to be actually paying attention to it.

"What position do you play, Mr. Short?" Geraldine asked.

Longarm gave her the standard lie about the sore shoulder that kept him from pitching.

Fancy, meanwhile, was looking over the visiting players like a matron in the butcher shop examining a tray of pork chops prior to making her selections.

"Who's that on first base?" she asked.

Longarm was paying more attention to Geraldine than to Fancy at the moment and only half heard. He thought she'd said something about that being Hoosier on first.

"That's right," he said.

"What?" Fancy asked.

"Levi . . . that's Watt's name . . . is on second."

Fancy blinked. Then shrugged. "And what's the name of that man over there on third base?"

"No, I already told you. Watt is on second." He glanced briefly toward the field. "The guy on third? I don't know."

"Thanks. I suppose."

Longarm didn't seem to be getting anywhere with Geraldine. And anyway his mind really wasn't focused on her. Nor on the ball game, for that matter.

He was really only waiting.

A couple innings later Jerry came running—or as close to it as he could manage—to fetch Longarm.

"The manager wants you to pinch hit now, Chet."

"Thanks, Jerry. Say, why don't you take my place answering these ladies' questions. Girls, this is Jerry. Ask him whatever you want to know. He knows more about this baseball club than anybody."

Jerry preened under Longarm's praise. Longarm was pretty sure he could come back any time that afternoon from now on and find Jerry glued to Fancy and Geraldine.

"If you'll excuse me now, ladies," he touched the brim of the stupid little cap, "I have some work t' do."

Chapter 48

What Longarm still couldn't figure out no matter how often he worried it over in his mind was: What did these baseball players find to be so difficult about taking a stick and hitting a ball?

It was a simple matter of hand and eye coordination. The eyes saw the ball coming. The hands whacked it with the stick. The ball flew into the air. Simple as that. Yet the ball players, guys who actually got paid real money for playing a kid's game, these guys made out like hitting the stupid ball was supposed to be difficult.

Even more amazing to them, most of these same fellows really couldn't hit a ball more than, say, one time in three or four. Hell, they even kept records of such things. Batting averages, they called it, although Longarm hadn't bothered to learn what was considered good and what was bad or how a batting average was arrived at.

He just wasn't that interested in keeping track of something so easy.

Now if these guys wanted difficult they should try shooting rabbits with a handgun while riding a running horse over rough ground.

That was difficult.

Hitting a thrown baseball was dead easy. All a fellow had to do was get the rhythm of the thing and let 'er rip.

Douglas McWhortle went out to tell the umpire that a pinch hitter would be coming in to replace Jason Hubbard and a man with a megaphone announced to the crowd that Chet Short would be batting.

Longarm found a reasonably clean towel to wipe his face and neck, lifted his cap to let a little air reach his scalp for half a second and then used the towel to swab off the grip of the bat he'd picked up.

Most of the boys were particular about what bats they used, but Longarm couldn't much tell one from another. He just picked up whichever one was closest to him. It kind of pissed some of the fellows off that his indifference worked so much better than their superior knowledge and general fussiness.

The Jonesboro pitcher, the third they'd used so far in the game, was a short, fat old boy who looked even hotter and more miserable in this weather than Longarm felt. Which hardly seemed possible but appeared to be true nonetheless.

Longarm took his place in the batter's box and stood there watching while the fat boy threw a few past him. He wanted to size up the aim and speed of the fat boy's throws before he hit the ball.

With the count at two balls and two strikes Longarm figured he'd better pay some attention this next toss. He waggled the bat a few times like he'd seen the others do, spat once for luck and waited.

The fat boy reared back and wound up like he was setting a spring, then flung the ball right down the middle.

Huh. It seemed hardly sporting the way the ball sailed along smooth and steady.

Longarm was in no hurry. He judged the timing of the throw, took half a step forward with his left foot ... and waled the bejabbers out of the horsehide.

The ball left the bat with a rather nicely satisfying crack and took off like it was fixing to punch holes in the nearest cloud.

No doubt about it. Longarm knew he had another of those home run hits before his bat ever connected. Hell, this one seemed high and far even to him.

There was a mighty groan from the crowd—it was natural enough that they would all be rooting for Jonesboro, all but a few locals who'd been sensible enough to place some money on the visiting professionals—and Longarm started to trot down to first base.

He wasn't halfway there when he heard the first gunfire from the direction of town.

One shot, two more close behind, and then a regular fusillade so thick and fast it was impossible to tell how many shots were fired.

Longarm sorted the sounds into categories. There were the sharp, light thumps of revolvers, a few cracks of rifle shots and, ending the fury, a succession of the dull booming reports of shotgun blasts.

Without needing to think about what had to be done he veered hard left and ran across the baseball diamond toward the refreshment canopy.

Chapter 49

As he'd expected, he found Jerry still hanging close to the ladies' skirts. The boy with the clubfoot looked worried.

"What was that, Chet? What's wrong?"

"It's okay if you want t' call me Longarm now, Jerry. The masquerade is over and I can be myself again."

"What's that? I don't understand."

Longarm shrugged and said, "That gunfire was your friends being brought to justice, Jerry. Either they're in custody or else they're dead. We'll know how it turned out when the town marshal gets here."

"I don't understand," Jerry repeated.

"Sorry, kid, but the game is over. Your pals are under arrest and now so are you."

"May I ask what this is about?" Fancy injected.

Longarm reached under his shirt and extracted the badge he'd been carrying—and none too comfortably either if the truth be told—hidden there since morning. "I'm a United States deputy marshal, ma'am. The name is Custis Long, not Chester Short. Sorry to've deceived you."

If anything Fancy looked rather pleased. Like she'd managed to count coup over her girlfriends who merely screwed baseball players while she had herself a real live federal lawman in the sack.

"Don't go sidling off like that, Jerry. You're under arrest, remember."

"I still don't . . ."

"Hell, boy, you tipped it off your own self the other day.

Remember back in Sorrel Branch when your buddies made their break after robbing the ticket booth? Afterward I got to asking myself a couple questions. One of them was why those boys, prepared as they obviously were, would bother to hit a lousy ticket booth when the pickings at the post office in town would certainly have been a hell of a lot better. Didn't make sense. Unless they somehow already knew there was an ambush waiting for them in that little no-law burg.

"Then I asked myself why a bunch of fleeing felons would go out of their way to detour through an alley and shoot hell out of the very bush I'd been sitting behind until the shooting tolled me out onto the street.

"The answers to both those questions just had t' come back to you, Jerry. After all, you're the only person in this whole wide world that knew the post office was being covered. And where I was setting t' do that job. Those friends of yours hit the booth because it wasn't guarded, and they swung by and tried to kill me so as to get me off their backs. And the only way they could have known to do either one of those things, Jerry, was if you told them to change the plan. Because you were the only one who *could* tell them."

"But I thought you agreed with me that no one could ride from Sorrel Branch to Jonesboro in time to pull a robbery here," Jerry said. "I thought you weren't expecting there to be any trouble here."

"I did tell you that, didn't I? When you kind of insisted that I come t' that conclusion. O' course what I remembered, an' I know you did too, is that if one bunch can take a train from Sorrel Branch to Jonesboro, so can another.

"I had my old friend Jonesboro Town Marshal Hugh Bullen watch the depot looking for three riders coming in. We didn't know what the men would look like since they'd been wearing those flour sack hoods back in Kansas, but I guess it must not've occurred to them that you can't hardly disguise a horse. I just told Hugh what horses t' look for, and the part about the riders just kinda fell into place along with those mounts.

"Your buddies unloaded just past dawn yesterday and went into camp a little while later. Some of Hugh's people been watching them day an' night since. And o' course your friends knew to place their ambush wherever I wasn't. Because that's where you would've told your gang to hit this time. I reckon if I'd stayed in town, your boys would've robbed the gate receipts again."

Longarm shrugged. "You almost got away with it, Jerry. Almost."

"You son of a bitch."

"Now, Jerry," Longarm admonished sadly. "You oughtn't to talk that way in front of ladies."

Jerry let out a sob. And lunged to grab Geraldine Flowers by the throat.

The boy pulled a tiny, nickel-plated revolver out of his pocket and shoved the muzzle into Geraldine's ear. "Don't make me shoot her, Longarm. I will if I have to. I swear that I will unless you back off and give me a fair start. Fair, that's all I'm asking. Just a head start."

Longarm sighed and shook his head. Why'd the stupid kid have to go and grab the pretty one, dammit. What a waste. This would have been easier if it was Fancy that Jerry was threatening.

"Kid, grow up, will you."

"I'll kill her, Longarm. I will."

"All right, Jerry. Then what will you do?"

Jerry blinked. "Huh?"

"What is it with you amateurs that you think taking a hostage makes you all of a sudden bulletproof? It was a simple question, kid. All it needs is a simple answer. So you have Miss Flowers for a hostage. You shoot her. So *then* what d'you do?"

Jerry looked confused by the question, simple or not.

"Look, kid, you can't accomplish much by shooting Miss Flowers. I mean, once you kill her you got no hostage any more, and I kill you in return. Sure she'd be dead but so would you. That's the trouble with a threat, son. You got no place to run once your bluff is called. Think about it. You can surrender to me nice and peaceable or you can kill Miss Flowers. Which I got to tell you would piss me off pretty thoroughly. If you do that I will shoot you dead just as sure as you and me are standing here. No, what you got to do, Jerry, is give yourself up. You'll get a fair trial and a prison term, but at least you'll still be alive when your time is done. You can get out and go make a start toward getting rich like you said you intended t' do." Longarm smiled gently. "Which, by the way, I understood at the time what you really meant. You were laughing up your sleeve at me, but I didn't mind. I knew Hugh and me had it under control."

"Damn you," Jerry moaned.

"Give it up, kid. Nice and peaceable."

"You're a nice lady," Jerry said to his hostage. "I'm sorry if I scared you. Longarm?"

"Yeah, kid?"

"You can't shoot me. Your gun is back in the boardinghouse. I'll let Miss Flowers go, but you got to let me get away. You just got to."

"Sorry, kid. I've already told you you're under arrest. That's the way we got to play it now."

Jerry bit at his underlip and seemed to think things over for several long seconds. Then he took his pistol away from the girl's head and gave her a little push in the back that sent her tottering into Fancy's arms a few paces away.

"Longarm, you got to promise me . . ."

"No, kid. I'm taking you in. All your chances are used up."

"Don't make me shoot you, Longarm. Please."

180

"Lay your gun down, Jerry. I'll see they treat you decent in jail."

The boy looked like he was fixing to cry.

But he wouldn't back down. He had gone too far now for that.

The muzzle of the little gun swung toward Longarm's chest and belly.

Longarm couldn't risk waiting any longer. The stupid kid hadn't been listening.

Or else maybe he had.

Either way, Longarm had no choice.

Longarm hooked the derringer out of his waistband where he'd been carrying it along with the badge.

The little .41 rimfire was small, but it packed man-sized power.

The report, exceptionally loud from such a short barrel, filled the space beneath the refreshment canopy to over-flowing.

And a small red indentation appeared, as if by magic, roughly in the center of young Jerry's forehead.

A pink mist filled the air behind him, and both Geraldine Flowers and Fancy screamed as the young robber gang baron collapsed in a heap like last week's soiled laundry.

Dammit, Longarm thought. Dammit anyway.

Behind him he could hear Douglas McWhortle and the manager of the Jonesboro team arguing about whether Longarm's homer should count since he hadn't completed running the base path.

Longarm hoped the two of them were able to work that out between them.

Personally he didn't much give a shit.

He turned and headed down the street toward town. He needed to see how Hugh and his people made out with the robbers, then he would have to get a wire off to Billy to tell the boss he was done playing children's games.

Dammit.

A special offer for people who enjoy reading the best Westerns published today.

WESTERNS!

NO OBLIGATION

Mail the coupon below

To start your subscription and receive 2 FREE WESTERNS, fill out the coupon below and mail it today. We'll send your first shipment which includes 2 FREE BOOKS as soon as we receive it.

Mail To: **True Value Home Subscription Services, Inc. P.O. Box 5235**
120 Brighton Road, Clifton, New Jersey 07015-5235

YES! I want to start reviewing the very best Westerns being published today. Send me my first shipment of 6 Westerns for me to preview FREE for 10 days. If I decide to keep them, I'll pay for just 4 of the books at the low subscriber price of $2.75 each; a total $11.00 (a $21.00 value). Then each month I'll receive the 6 newest and best Westerns to preview Free for 10 days. If I'm not satisfied I may return them within 10 days and owe nothing. Otherwise I'll be billed at the special low subscriber rate of $2.75 each; a total of $16.50 (at least a $21.00 value) and save $4.50 off the publishers price. There are never any shipping, handling or other hidden charges. I understand I am under no obligation to purchase any number of books and I can cancel my subscription at any time, no questions asked. In any case the 2 FREE books are mine to keep.

Name _____

Street Address _____ Apt. No. _____

City _____ State _____ Zip Code _____

Telephone _____

Signature _____
(if under 18 parent or guardian must sign)

Terms and prices subject to change. Orders subject
to acceptance by True Value Home Subscription
Services, Inc.

11861-3